W9-BQI-273

GET THE SHOW ON THE ROAD - "A 'feel good' story that shows a different and refreshing twist to black romance fiction. Good reading for the young at heart, but required reading for those who want to stereotype Blacks and emasculate the strong African-American male role model outside of Sports and Entertainment."
__*Atlanta Daily World,* Atlanta, Georgia

"It should be mandated by the law of the land that everyone read **GET THE SHOW ON THE ROAD by Evelyn Allen Johnson,** for it will be an everlasting experience."
__*The Birmingham Times/The Western Times,* Birmingham, Alabama

"**GET THE SHOW ON THE ROAD** is a story full of love, hope and inspiration, so skillfully woven with emotion, humor, passion and surprise that one can't put it down until finished. Readers need more books like this!" __*Herald-Dispatch, Los Angeles, CA*

GET THE SHOW ON THE ROAD - "A book that paints positive images of African men and women, especially the men, is worth its weight in gold."
"Finally, a novel that doesn't sell Blacks out as buffoons or sexual deviants"
"*EVELYN ALLEN JOHNSON* weaves a colorful love story of black passion and romance." __*Los Angeles Watts Times, Los Angeles, CA*

GET THE SHOW ON THE ROAD is a must read. A modern day love story that paints a positive picture of African-American relationships. Evelyn Allen Johnson has outdone herself. __*The New Pittsburgh Courier, Pittsburgh, PA*

GET THE SHOW ON THE ROAD

Evelyn Allen Johnson

A Lynray Press Book

To Mary Evans!
with my most
best wishes, Always!
Evelyn
Thanks to your
husband, Tom!
6/6/99

A Lynray Press Book
Copyright © 1987 by Evelyn Allen Johnson

Library of Congress Catalog Card Number: 94-075577

ISBN 0-9640326-0-0

Manufactured in the United States of America

Second Edition: April 1998

For information write to:

Lynray Press
3756 Santa Rosalia Drive Suite #220
Los Angeles, CA 90008

Cover design by Kevin Allen Pike

To the loving memory of dear
Aunt Jennie Bynum Latta Peirce
and to
Michael
for his Love and Devotion to her

A new perspective in similarity. . .

GET THE SHOW ON THE ROAD

GET THE SHOW ON THE ROAD

Evelyn Allen Johnson

A Lynray Press Book

CHAPTER 1

t had been raining all morning, and now the sun was trying its best to shine. The air was fresh. Two days of rain had washed away the smog. The palm trees swayed and waved skyward, thankful that the rainy season had arrived and their thirst of months would be quenched. The traffic was slow, and ambulance sirens screamed loudly, all over the city, as they rushed auto accident victims to the nearest hospitals. This was not unusual at the start of the season. For months Los Angeles streets and freeways had collected oil from millions of vehicles, and now this mixture of oil and water made a slick as hazardous as ice for many motorists.

The Rapid Transit Bus, which seemed to have taken hours to reach its destination, stopped at

1

the corner of Washington and La Brea. A lithe, young woman dressed in a yellow rain slicker, white nurse's oxfords, and white stockings jumped agilely onto the side walk avoiding the rushing gully water, as it poured downward to flood the next intersection. She carried an armful of heavy textbooks and a yellow umbrella. Looking into that pretty face one could quickly discern anxiety. She didn't want to be late, which she already was, and she was trying to memorize the fetal heart circulation, which was certain to be on the Pediatric midterm tomorrow morning.

Africa Jones' body moved quickly forward, as her strong, shapely legs kept up an almost running gait. The yellow rain hood bounced on her shoulders, and served as a receptacle for the thick, almost black, wavy hair that filled it.

I've got to get out of there earlier, but I get so involved, she thought. If only she could just go to school, become a Registered Nurse, and forget this job. She was up at five thirty every morning, so that she could get to her eight o'clock class, then she had to rush away at three to be on the job by four. This was an exciting last year, and she would often get so absorbed with her classes or patients that she couldn't break away in time. Miss Thornton, the Director of Nurses at the New Hope Convalescent

Hospital where she worked, had told her that just one more time and she was through. But surely today with the rain and traffic she would understand, Africa felt.

Oh Lord, she thought, please let her understand. Mama, Billy, and Brenda were counting on her, and they just wouldn't be able to make it if she lost her job. A lock of hair fell over her eye, but she couldn't free an arm to brush it away. It was always annoying when her hair got in the way. For that reason, and because she was usually in uniform, Africa pinned it back into a soft bun. Evidently, when the hood slipped from her head, it had loosened her hair. Now she would have to take extra time to put her appearance in order. She cringed thinking about Miss Thornton and what a stickler she was when adhering to the dress code. It was indeed stressful having a rigid disciplinarian breathing down your neck all the time. Africa knew she wasn't one of her favorite persons. At last she neared the hospital. Maybe, I'll only be ten minutes late and they'll still be in report she thought. If so, I can just stand in the hallway by the door and she won't know when I came in. She was now pleased that the room in which the change of shift report was given was too small to hold everyone inside, and some of the nurses always remained in the doorway.

With this new surge of hope, Africa's face brightened. Her dark eyes seemed to glow in her chocolate colored skin, which had a texture so smooth and soft that the finest velvet would appear coarse in comparison. A speck of a mole, just above her left upper lip, was truly a beauty mark. With renewed energy, she darted up the broad cement stairs of the hospital entrance, taking them two at a time. She tried to glance at her watch, then bam! There was a strong resistance and she realized that she had collided with another being. She watched in dismay as her thick, eighty-six dollar, surgical textbook slid down the rain soaked stairs. Somebody said, "Shit!" She realized it was her, and with tremendous embarrassment as she stared into the face of the young man, who had jumped around her, retrieved the book, and now placed it back on it's perch, atop the others he held.

"Now, that's a heavy one," he said with a smile. "I'm really very sorry."

"It's O.K. I'm sorry too. I don't usually curse like that, but I'm late and this book is rather expensive."

His good looks stunned her. Evidently, he was equally effected by her, because they stood as if

4

electrified, staring at one another until a sharp, brittle voice brought them back to reality.

"Kevin, will you come, now! I don't have time for any nonsense!" spoke the female owner of the voice. She was tall, thin and almost white. She grabbed him by the arm, and tugged with agitation, as she passed on her way down the steps.

"The bank closes at four-thirty, and your Father wants me to make some deposits for him. Come on. I can't be held up with a lot of foolishness." She fussed all the way to the sidewalk.

"Thank you." managed Africa.

"You work here?" he asked, apparently ignoring the woman, as he observed Africa's white shoes, stockings and as she well knew, her legs, because his eyes smiled a big approval.

It took her a second to come back to earth.

"You work here?" he repeated. He was no longer smiling, and there was a seriousness and urgency in his voice that compelled her to answer.

"I'm not sure, that is, after today. You see I'm late". She felt breathless.

"Kevin! Come on!" The voice came again, this time from the window of the Mercedes parked at the curb.

"All right, Mother. On my way!" He turned quickly back to Africa. "You've got to have a beautiful name".

"Africa, Africa Jones," she said and darted up the steps.

"I knew it was a pretty one", he called as she disappeared inside the heavy double doors.

Once inside, Africa greeted the patients sitting in the comfortable lobby with exhilaration. They were mostly elderly, but there were some in their forties and a few others still younger. They eagerly returned her greeting. Africa was one of their favorites. She was on a high. Generally she was bright and cheerful, but the brief encounter she had just experienced transported her aloft to the clouds. The day was no longer dreary and rainy. Instead she felt bright and sunny. The weight of her earlier worries was lifted, and she was no longer bothered by thoughts of Miss Thornton or her exams tomorrow. She felt a beautiful warmth, just recalling the young man, his handsomeness, and the fact that he was so struck by her that he had to have her name and know if she worked here.

Oh, I will see him again, she thought, and there was a sudden spring in her step, and a quickening of her pulses. She looked radiant.

"Better hurry, Africa, Thornton's having her monthly staff meeting, and they haven't started report yet."

It was Chuck Wilson, the Hospital Administrator. He was forty, pudgy, rich and in love with Africa. His family owned a chain of convalescent hospitals, and New Hope was one of them. His father had sent him to New Hope to clean it up, since things were in a mess during the last administration. Now that he had straightened everything out, and the Health Department was off the company's back, he could have left at any time, but didn't want to do so without first making Africa his wife.

She didn't know the depth of his feelings for her, but considered him a good friend since he kept Miss Thornton from firing her.

"I'm in luck", she answered breathlessly and with a smile.

She rushed down the cheery corridor, with its murals of flower gardens and with lattices covered with budding vines, then quickly disappeared into Room Sixteen. No time for the locker room, she thought.

"Hi," she called entering the room.

Mrs. Lottie Hildenbrandt was propped up in bed, as usual, reading. The older woman raised her snow white head and peered over her glasses. A happy smile spread over her aristocratic, brown features when she recognized Africa.

"All right, come on in and leave your things on the chair. It's behind the door. I've been expecting you. Better hurry, you don't want to be too late. I hear Thornton's been on the rampage today, all day!"

Africa was out of her yellow slicker in a flash. Mrs. Hildenbrandt was one of her favorite patients, and her confidante.

The old lady had been in New Hope for five years, and had celebrated her eighty-sixth birthday a week ago. She was paralyzed from the waist down and had an arrested case of cancer. At least it was quiet, with no signs of growth, and she suffered little pain. The plump matriarch was an avid reader, and among many personal items in her room were scores of books, stacked in bookcases, which had been installed along the walls at her direction. She could move the upper portion of her body like a dynamo, and resembled an octopus as she puttered in the many receptacles that sat on stands placed in close proximity to her bed. A bed that she refused to leave. During her confinement at New Hope, she had only left her room one time and had been out of bed only three times, the last time being six months ago, and at Africa's insistence. The girl was her favorite and the only one who could successfully turn her mattress without her having to leave the bed, an accomplishment which had been taught Africa by her mother, Lucy, who also used to work at the hospital. Mrs. Hildenbrandt insisted upon Africa being assigned to her. Since she was a private patient, and widow of the founding president of the Quality Mutual Savings and Loan Institution, first and largest black banking institution west of Chicago, and the Western Mutual Insurance Co., her wishes were granted.

Africa's face was radiant as she quickly twisted her thick dark hair and held it in place at the back of her head. Reaching towards Mrs. Hildenbrandt, she asked, "Please, may I borrow a hair pin? I've lost mine."

"Child, you'll be the death of me yet", exclaimed Mrs. Hildenbrandt as she furiously searched in a china container and promptly produced the pin.

"Thanks. Remind me to tell you about something wonderful that happened to me today," whispered Africa as she quickly departed the room. Mrs. Hildenbrandt smiled. She noticed the excitement about Africa, and knew it wasn't just due to her rush. The girl was her contact with interest in the outside world. In all her years, Mrs. Hildenbrandt had seen many beautiful women, but in her opinion, Africa was the Queen of them all. This was not just because of her physical attributes, which were indeed rare, but also because of her lovely personality. She found the girl to be sweet, unselfish, brilliant, and totally unaffected by her striking beauty. Africa's optimism and zest for living brought Mrs. Hildenbrandt new life. She liked to imagine the girl as the daughter or granddaughter she never had.

Luck was with Africa. She made it to the Conference room just in time to stand outside a few minutes with some other late comers, she being the latest. Mrs. Thornton was busy lecturing on bedsores, her pet peeve. For good reason, because any sore that developed in the facility would cost the owners one thousand dollars, and her a raise. The Health Department was a stringent monitor.

"A decubitus means only one thing. Poor nursing care! Any nurse who lets one develop, will be fired. I will not tolerate poor nursing care. Now don't think I can't pinpoint the shift on which it occurs. I haven't been in this business thirty-five years for nothing," lectured the director. Miss Thornton was a stern faced, tall, angular woman, somewhere in her early sixties. She always wore a spotless, white uniform, with an impressive white cap bearing two black bands, perched high upon her mixed gray, neatly coiffure head. She insisted that her nursing staff look just as neat as herself, and she set a fine example for them to follow. She had been known to provide uniforms for new girls, just starting, and permit them to wait on their first pay check before buying one, in case they were short on money. Only one quarter of her staff were licensed nurses, and she required that each wear their cap. Those caps worn by the Practical Nurses were plain, while the Registered Nurses' caps bore one black band. As a nurses' aide, Africa didn't wear a cap. She could hardly wait until she graduated and passed her state board examinations, so that she could don the coveted white cap with a black band.

"Meeting dismissed!, barked Miss Thornton. "Now all you evening nurses come on in here, and get a quick report from the day crew. We're a little late getting started, so step lively!"

Miss Thornton watched Africa as the girl took her seat. Africa knew the woman was wishing she knew just when she came on duty, since she hadn't been inside the room. Miss Thornton didn't like Africa, and the girl knew that she intended to carry out her threat to fire her, just as soon as she had enough ammunition for the administrator to buy. It didn't matter that Africa was a good aide. She refused to make allowances, even though Africa was a student at the state college, and would soon obtain her Bachelor of Science Degree in Nursing. She felt the girl was too pretty to be successful as a nurse, and considered her a threat. This was a conclusion some of Africa's co-workers had derived from conversations with the woman, and told to Africa, when they observed the unfair treatment she received on a daily basis. Others felt it was because of Miss Thornton's disappointment, and the fact that she couldn't stand to see any one happy most of the time, as Africa always seemed to be.

As the story went, Miss Thornton was an old army nurse. Early in her army career, she had been engaged to a very handsome, young physician, who was also an officer. They were very much in love. Two days before their marriage, he was killed, when the army hospital was bombed. He died in her arms, and Miss Thornton had never been the same since. After her retirement from the service, she had taken a position at New Hope. She wore her former fiancé's picture in a locket under her uniform, and on occasion would show it to some of the other nurses. She lived alone, and New Hope was her only interest.

GET THE SHOW ON THE ROAD

Miss Thornton knew that Chuck Wilson, the administrator, was in love with Africa, and it was only because of his interference that she had not been able to terminate the girl. It seemed he had already suggested to her that she make Africa her assistant after she obtained her degree. Miss Thornton didn't want an assistant, and she liked her work too much to even think about a second retirement. She was watching Africa closely, however she didn't worry too much about what time the girl had arrived on duty, because she knew she would find out soon. She had a system, which allowed her to know anything she wanted to know that concerned New Hope.

Africa was quite busy all evening. She had five patients to feed, and ten to make ready for bed. That included diapering several, not mention the turning and changes in between. Just getting her wheel chair patients in bed took a great deal of time. Then there was the new admission, a beautiful, thirty-two year old, gunshot victim whose husband had caught her in bed with her lover. The husband killed him, but the young woman survived a bullet wound in the head. She was paralyzed from the neck down. The acute hospital had sent her to New Hope, and Africa knew this was likely to be her home for the rest of her life. Her name was Peggy, and she was quite depressed. Africa spent as much time as possible trying to take care of her needs, and cheer her. As a matter of fact, she even gave Peggy her two fifteen minute break periods. She ate a quick lunch, while scanning her textbook. Africa always brought a sandwich and salad locked in a plastic macramé bag, which her Mother had made for that purpose. Usually she would put them in the locker room refrigerator, but today, she had been so rushed, she had forgotten.

Africa always seemed to lose herself in her work, but tonight was special. The handsome face of the young man she had collided with on the hospital's front steps, kept surfacing before her. Just thinking of him brought a special sort of warmth rushing all over her, and she would move quickly with excitement.

I must see him again, I must, she thought over and over as she performed her duties with extra special zeal, which further cheered and endeared her patients.

Mrs. Hildenbrandt watched her favorite television program, while Africa gave her a good back rub and straightened her bed. Africa had planned to come back later for her usual chat, but then she became too busy, and had a mountain of charting to finish. When she finally tiptoed back into Mrs. Hildenbrandt's room, to say good night, the old lady was sound asleep. It was after eleven p.m. Africa turned off the television, made certain the call light was pinned to the pillow, and cut off the light. She left the bathroom door ajar, so that it's light made a small pathway into the room. This was the way Mrs. Hildenbrandt liked it. After picking up the remainder of her belongings from the chair behind the door, Africa quietly left the old lady snoring.

Outside the building, Billy waited for Africa. He was her younger brother. Each night she worked, he was there waiting for her. Their mother insisted, and even if Billy had fallen asleep, she awakened him to pull on his pants, and go meet Africa. He carried a thirty-eight caliber pistol in his pocket. It was too dangerous for a young woman to walk the streets alone at that time of night. Two girls who worked with Africa had been forced into cars, taken away, robbed and raped, within the past few months, therefore, Lucy, their mother, was taking no chances.

Billy was a high school senior, looking forward to going away to college on a football scholarship. His long range goal and dream was to become a lawyer. Africa and Lucy kept on him constantly about his studies, and he was a much

15

better than average student. A fine looking young man with black curly hair and a serious expression on his clean cut features, he was quite popular with the girls. Billy made a heroic, he-man picture on the playing field. For this reason, his mother and sisters reminded him almost daily to keep girls at a distance, particularly if he wanted a career.

The two walked quickly, amid drizzling rain, the few blocks home. They discussed briefly their busy day, but Africa left out the thrilling encounter which brightened hers. Even Billy noticed her extra cheerfulness. He thought it unusual, since she had mentioned she would be up late tonight preparing for two heavy exams tomorrow. They entered the kitchen door at the side of the house, so as to not awaken Lucy, who slept on the hide-a-bed in the living room. They were barely inside, when as usual, Lucy called out to them.

"Billy! Africa! That you?"

"Hi Mom! It's us!" called Africa.

"Thank God", said Lucy, and promptly fell back asleep. This had become a ritual on the nights Africa worked.

It had been six years since the children's father, Lucy's husband, died as the result of an automobile accident. Lucy took it very hard, and mourned him to the extent of wearing black for six months. She and Leroy had been a devoted and as near perfect couple as one could ever hope to meet.

The car was demolished, and Lucy did not have the money to replace it. Leroy was in the process of changing over to a cheaper insurance, when the accident occurred.

"I love you, Lucy. Take care of the kids. Just my luck", these were his dying words to Lucy at the hospital. She was sorry she had once accused him of being insurance poor, because his foresight turned out to be a blessing. She may have lost out on the car, due to Leroy's desire to change policies, but the other insurance policies he managed to keep up, paid for their little house. Then, all Lucy had to do was to try and manage on the Nurses' Aide salary she was making at New Hope. She had managed to get Leroy's approval to work there part time, three years before his death, when the Wilson family had bought the Hospital. She was a highly respected employee, however, several months after Leroy's death, she developed fear and anxiety so intense, she was unable to leave home. Even a trip to the corner grocery store became an impossibility. The last time she left home, she had gone to the supermarket where she developed such anxiety that she cringed in a corner, shook and cried so that the paramedics had to be called, and she was hospitalized. The physicians diagnosed her malady, agoraphobia, and sent her home. She had not left the house since, and could venture safely only to the far limits of their back yard. Her fears extended to include her children, and she worried about them constantly when they were away from home.

Mr. Wilson hired Africa in her Mother's place when the girl finished high school. She was given an on the job training period, and small salary, which was indispensable to the household. Africa decided she must become a Registered Nurse, and have a college degree. She passed all the pre-entrance examinations, and was thrilled when accepted into the Nursing Program at California State University. This was now her fifth and last year. Because she had to work, it had taken her an extra year, but Africa had made it with the help of merit scholarships and Lucy's encouragement.

Billy took the gun from his pocket, and placed it in the cake holder atop the refrigerator.

"Night, Africa", he called from the hall on his way to his bedroom.

"Night," she seemed to sing to him, as she spread her books on the kitchen table in preparation for a night of study.

It was three in the morning when Lucy came into the kitchen and found Africa still studying. She made quite a fuss, and to quiet her, Africa closed her books, kissed Lucy, and staggered across the living room to the bedroom which she shared with her older sister, Brenda, and Brenda's illegitimate, fourteen month old Joey. They were both sleeping soundly, and Africa didn't wish to awaken the baby. He would be awake and yelling soon enough. Six in the morning was his time to start the day, and he was so regular, they didn't need an alarm clock. Africa slipped out of her uniform, and then into the empty twin bed. Brenda turned over in the next bed, but did not awaken. Adjusting her pillow for comfort, Africa felt a lump, and recognized it as a small wad of bills. Suddenly she remembered that Brenda's welfare check would have come today, and since Africa paid all the utility bills, this was Brenda's share. Africa felt sorry for her sister, and swore for the several thousandth time, that she would never end up in her fix. No life of welfare checks for her. A feeling of warmth and sweetness flooded over her again, as the face of the young man on the steps engulfed her memory. She fell asleep confident that she would see him again, and that he would play an important role in her life.

CHAPTER 2

wo weeks passed swiftly, Africa's midterms were behind her. She passed all her courses, and maintained a "B" average. Her days remained on the same routine, but she felt satisfaction in the knowledge that soon, she would reach her goal.

For a reason she couldn't fathom, the handsome young man she bumped into on New Hope's front steps, still occupied her thoughts. She had not told anyone about him, deciding to savor the sweetness of her secret alone for a day or two. Usually, she would confide in Mrs. Hildenbrandt her cherished tidbits, but since she had not had time the first two days following the incident, she found it more difficult to mention as the days passed. Actually, because she had not seen him again, and he had obviously made no attempt to contact her, she did not wish to risk being thought of as ridiculous. It had to sound silly, she thought, because she didn't even know his last name, and only thought she knew his first by having heard his mother call to him. He had apparently forgotten all about her the minute he drove away in that shiny, new Mercedes.

After ten days, she really felt stupid when she caught herself thinking of him. In an effort to erase his memory, she accepted Chuck Wilson's invitation to dine with him and see a movie. Africa had told her mother about her upcoming date with Chuck. Lucy was terribly excited, asking her daughter what she planned to wear, telling her what would be the best things to talk about, and how she should act, walk and even smile.

"Please, Mom, I'm not trying to marry him. I'm just going out on a friendly date."

"Well, you'd better think about marriage, Africa, if you can get him. His family is loaded and you'd be putting yourself on easy street. Chuck Wilsons don't come along but once in a lifetime!"

"Oh, Mom!"

"Oh Mom, nothing girl. I'm just trying to talk some sense into your head. I want you to have some of the good life. I don't want you to be like

Brenda, stuck with a child, and a no good clown like Moses, who won't marry her cause she'll lose her welfare check. That no good rascal came sneaking round here a couple of nights ago, and I had to threaten to blow his head off."

"Mom, please, Brenda might hear you. Remember, we promised not to make her feel bad."

"All right, Honey, all right", said Lucy, unable to hide her shame.

Africa quickly left the house to do the grocery shopping. Just as soon as Lucy knew she was gone, she rushed to check out her daughter's wardrobe, but couldn't find a thing suitable for Africa to wear. Finally, she went to the hall closet, where she kept her clothing. There she decided upon a most cherished item. A red suit, which Leroy had bought for her as a birthday gift. It was the most expensive she had ever owned, made of a very lightweight wool, with exquisite detail. Of course, Lucy was a size fourteen, and Africa wore a size seven, but Lucy's greatest talent was sewing. She took the suit to her machine, in the little dining room, and began working. After all, she wasn't ever going anywhere so what did she need with the suit. If it helped Africa get Chuck Wilson, then her sacrifice would pay off generously.

Lucy finished the suit just in time for Africa to dress. She met some resistance, at first, when she suggested to her daughter what she should wear, but after Africa tried on the suit, there were no further complaints.

Lucy had made it into a smart gored mini skirt, which clung to Africa's curvaceous hips and thighs in a most tantalizing manner. She wore a black satin blouse with a high neck of ruffles, and a string of pearls with matching earrings. Black high heeled boots added the fantastic finishing touch Lucy wanted. Africa smiled with satisfaction at her image in the hallway's full length mirror. Her mane of dark hair was striking with the red. Lucy knew that anyplace Africa went tonight, all eyes would be upon her. She watched when Africa greeted Chuck in their living room. He stuttered, stammered and was almost speechless. When they walked out to his new Seville Cadillac, Lucy was ecstatic, because she knew Africa was the most beautiful and sexy female he had ever dated. She felt certain that after tonight Africa's future would be secure. She even imagined what she would wear to the wedding. Even if it killed her, she would leave the house on that day.

Dinner at the exclusive Marina City Club was delightful. Chuck was an excellent conversationalist, and he laughed often at his own jokes, while dabbing his mustached mouth with the white linen napkin. Africa refused more than one glass of wine, because this was always stated with emphasis in Lucy's instructions.

"A girl has to keep her head. Drinking's what got most gals into trouble. Lowers your resistance and you might lose your virginity to the wrong man. Ask Brenda. That was Moses' biggest trick. After a few drinks that fool knowed she'd be seeing him looking like Billy Dee."

Africa decided, long ago, that she wanted to keep her head, and not make any mistakes. She became more and more disenchanted with Chuck as she watched him eat.

No wonder he's overweight. He really pigs out, she thought. Fat men just don't have sex appeal, she concluded again as she had many times before when considering Chuck. It was then her mind wandered to the young man on the steps.

"Everything all right, Africa?" asked Chuck. "You look as if you're a million miles away."

Africa felt guilty as she said, "Oh, no. I was thinking about the point you just made." Then Chuck started again with renewed enthusiasm to reinforce his statement. He kept the conversation at a lively, one sided pace through out the remainder of their meal.

At one point he mentioned her work at New Hope.

"You like working at the hospital, don't you, Africa?"

"Oh, yes," she answered.

"I notice old lady Hildenbrandt is one of your favorites. Seems you really dig them old folks."

"I like old people. You can learn so much from them, and some are really cute. Mrs. Hildenbrandt is a dear."

"I hate suffering," commented Chuck. "Some ought just be allowed to die without a lot of messing around, IVs, tubes and all that stuff. When they can't eat, they just ought to be allowed to go ahead and die."

Africa thought, that's because you like eating so much, but she said, "Maybe you're right, Chuck, but I feel life is sacred and everything should be done to preserve it. That's why I don't believe in abortion, euthanasia or anything like that."

"You're a good little nurse," Chuck managed between chuckles and bites.

"I hope to be," said Africa.

The after dinner movie was a comedy, during which Chuck would intermittently roar with laughter. Africa tried laughing with him but didn't think the scenes were all that funny. An uneasiness crept over her when he put his arm around the back of her seat, and then during each fit of laughter would squeeze her tight, dropping popcorn in her lap. But the last straw was when he squeezed her knee, and then after the laughter was over, he never removed his hand. She remedied the situation by excusing herself to go to the ladies room.

After the movie, he insisted on stopping by his apartment, overlooking the ocean. Africa didn't complain since she was curious to see the apartment of which he so frequently spoke with pride. She accepted his invitation to have a light snack.

Africa really wanted to like Chuck more, if for no other reason than to please Lucy. Inside his lavishly furnished living room, Chuck stepped behind his red and black mirrored bar, fixed himself a drink, and turned on his elaborate stereo set. Africa refused a cocktail, but he made her a scotch and milk anyway. She pretended to sip it, but knew the potted plant next to her would get nourished that evening. Neither was she hungry, so she watched Chuck devour a healthy corned beef sandwich he had quickly thrown together in his well equipped kitchen. She felt it would be a joy to live in such a beautiful, modernistic apartment, but she couldn't imagine sharing it with Chuck.

It wasn't long before he settled onto the plush, red velvet play pen with her. He had been steadily asking her about tasting her drink, and now half of it was gone. The milk plant at her side was living up to it's name. When he kissed her, she tried to respond, but the harshness of his mouth and the brutal force with which he held her became frightening. His hand felt hot on her thigh, as he progressively kneaded her tender flesh. His breathing was becoming heavy and raspy. His other hand began to fondle her breast, as he pushed his tongue deeper into her mouth. She felt saliva drool on her chin amid the smell of onions and corned beef.

Suddenly, she was struggling, breaking away from his embraces, and crying, "Stop it! Stop it!"

Chuck looked at her with surprise, as she jumped to her feet, straightening her skirt.

"What is it? What's the matter?" he asked, dumbfounded.

"Chuck, please don't get offended. I'm sorry, but I'm, well I'm scared".

"Scared? Honey, I wouldn't hurt you."

"I know, Chuck," she lied. "But I'm, well, I've never ..."

Chuck laughed, cutting her off, "Africa, you mean you're a virgin?" He paused for a moment, staring at her. "I should have known it, but I didn't think there were any more of those around these days."

"Please, Chuck, take me home. My Mom's gonna be worried, it's two a.m."

Africa grabbed her black purse from the coffee table.

"O.K., Honey. O.K. Don't get so excited. I guess Mrs. Jones is concerned. You are indeed her little, innocent daughter."

Africa stood by the door. Chuck came to her, and kissed her hard on the lips. She imagined they were swelling.

"Africa, Honey, you gotta know I love you. I have for a long time. After tonight, I love you more than ever, if that's possible. I want you to marry me, Girl. Now you think about that. You can have everything I've got. I'm offering it to you, Baby. Promise me you'll think about it."

It was Africa's turn to be surprised.

"Chuck, I didn't know. I don't know what to say."

"Don't say a thing. Just promise me you'll think about it."

"Of course, Chuck. I will. I'll give it serious thought", she said, looking into his soulful eyes which were on the same level as her own.

He pulled her close to him and kissed her again.

Driving home, he held his right hand over hers, while driving, squeezing it intermittently as he talked about his family, how much she would like them, and his plans for their future. He, eventually, wanted to make her Supervising Nurse over all their Convalescent Hospitals. Africa felt sick as he kissed her again at her door, this time on her cheek. She felt sick, because she knew she would never again go out with Chuck Wilson, and she would never be in love with him.

CHAPTER 3

he Monday morning following her date with Chuck, Africa felt a weight of depression. It was a five minute walk from the time she alighted from the bus, until she reached the impressive building, which housed the School of Nursing. Once inside, she took her seat in the Critical Care Class, awaiting the instructor's arrival. She was a few minutes early. The classroom buzzed with conversation in which she was usually engaged, but today, she withdrew herself pretending to read notes of previous lectures. She thought about how upset Lucy was with her when she told her she would never date Chuck Wilson again.

Lucy wanted to know what had happened, and she told her, "Nothing. He just proposed to me."

What?" Lucy cried. "And you tell me you'll never go out with him again. Africa, you can't mean that!" Lucy began to talk so fast, she nearly choked on her grapefruit. After a paroxysm of coughing, which required the assistance of Billy and Brenda, as well as Africa, to control with slaps on the back, sips of water, and help in wiping the tears of strain and anguish from her eyes, she was able to tell Africa only in a whisper, how crazy she was.

Brenda agreed with Lucy, and only Billy stood up for Africa. "She don't have to marry anybody she don't love, money or no money. I don't blame her one damn bit! Anybody can see Chuck Wilson's too old for her. He ain't her type at all, so why don't you all just leave her alone!"

In between her religious programs on television, Lucy fussed all day, telling Africa she didn't know what love was. She described it as security, money in your purse, ready to spend, and not having to work your butt off every day. The only peace Africa had was when she took little Joey for a walk. It was the longest they had ever taken, and she finally brought him home sound asleep in his stroller.

With a start, Africa abandoned her day dreaming becoming aware that the instructor had arrived, and was reviewing several basic types of electrocardiogram strips. Realizing that his was a difficult and vital class, she quickly buried her thoughts, and gave Miss Watson her full attention. It was fortunate for Africa that she loved nursing. Because of this interest, she was able to tune out her depression, and that afternoon, at Mercy Hospital, where she and other classmates did their practical work, she was a source of cheer to her patients. There was a great deal of pleasant camaraderie between all the students. Africa was outgoing and well liked by her peers. She was pleased that the afternoon passed quickly, and that she had enjoyed it so much.

Africa arrived five minutes early for work at New Hope. Chuck stepped out of his office and waved to her, as she passed quickly in the corridor adjacent to his office. She could see he did not wish to broadcast his involvement with her, and she was pleased, because under the circumstances, it could cause a difficult situation for her. First, it would be quite unprofessional, and secondly, it would necessitate a confrontation with him earlier than she desired. She hoped she could cool him off, by being busy, distant, and never alone with him. It was good that he left at five every day.

Miss Thornton gave Africa an icy stare, as she passed the nurses' station, on her way to the locker room. The director noted that the girl's uniform seemed to accentuate her innocent, but definite sexiness. There were no grounds on which she could complain. The shoes were brightly white, so was the uniform, which just fit her well, but wasn't too tight. Africa was definitely within the dress codes, and Miss Thornton finally came to her usual conclusion that Africa would be beautiful in a burlap sack. On the other hand, Africa was aware of Miss Thornton's scrutiny, and was happy that she also left around five.

Africa had twenty patients. Nine of them were helpless, and required turning every hour, in order to prevent the dreaded bedsores. Four of the nine were comatose. Two others were hopelessly senile and so contracted in their musculature, that they could not move. Among the remaining, were Peggy, the gunshot victim, and Mrs. Hildenbrandt, whose turning was a joke. This was so because the old lady would never permit herself to be turned. Instead, she managed to bend and contort until she massaged those threatened portions of her own body frequently enough to keep the blood circulating, thus preventing bedsores from developing. Even though she had been on her back for five and one half years, her skin was smooth and healthy. At night, it was her ritual to apply a special cream which she mixed periodically herself. She had given Africa a jar, which the girl used occasionally, particularly when she remembered Mrs. Hildenbrandt saying,

"Now, my dear, you don't wait until the wrinkles appear. Then, it is too late. You start now. My mother started me on this treatment when I was fifteen years old." To make emphasis, she dragged the words "years old" in her special proper way.

"I'm eighty-six now, and how many wrinkles do you see?"

It was fantastic. Mrs. Hildenbrandt had a smooth wrinkle free face. There was a little sagging, and dark circles around her eyes, but no wrinkles.

Africa always saved Mrs. Hildenbrandt's care until last, since this would enable her to linger a few minutes with her dear friend. It was after dinner, and Africa was helping Mrs. Hildenbrandt prepare for visitors. She rarely had any, but this evening was special, because she was expecting a relative who had called just an hour earlier to say he had arrived in town.

As it frequently occurred, both were laughing while the older woman told Africa an anecdote from the days of her school teaching experience. There were certain children whom Africa had grown to know quite well, and the older woman never tired of talking about them. Sometimes when Africa needed a boost, she would step inside the room for a few moments, and become rejuvenated by one of Mrs. Hildenbrandt's humorous yarns.

Africa had just finished helping Mrs. Hildenbrandt into a lovely ice blue, satin gown, trimmed in the most delicate of ivory lace. Mrs. Hildenbrandt sprayed on a touch of her very expensive, imported parfum, then asked Africa to retrieve an ivory comb to place in her hair.

Africa opened the drawer, then paused. She was clearly shocked, and for a second appeared dazed.

"What is it, Child?" asked Mrs. Hildenbrandt.

Africa reached in the drawer, and brought out a photograph of four persons. Two, she recognized, the young man of her dreams and the woman he called Mother.

"Who is this?" she asked, pointing to the younger man.

"That's Kevin, my grandson. Why? What's wrong?" Mrs. Hildenbrandt pointed to the picture as Africa continued to stare.

"That's him, his mother, and his father, who is my son, and that girl standing next to him, looking right silly, is his girlfriend, Nanette." The girl didn't look silly to Africa. She seemed quite attractive.

"You've heard me talk about them, Africa. He do something to you, or what?"

"No, no, not really. I just can't believe it!"

"Can't believe it?"

"Yes," said Africa, as she looked at the picture and began to smile.

"Well, come on now, Child, what's going on here?" asked Mrs. Hildenbrandt as she relaxed back into her pillows.

It was then that Africa related her experience with Kevin.

"I didn't tell you about it before because I didn't want you to think I was going off the deep end, particularly since I've not seen him since. And now to make everything completely a wreck, he has a girlfriend!"

"Well, he is in good health, Dear. What would you expect? She's not the first, and I doubt she'll be the last. Rather, I hope she won't be anyway," sighed Mrs. Hildenbrandt.

"You don't like her?" Africa's eyes brightened.

"No. I can't stand her, but I'm not going to go into that. Maybe I don't have good reasons, just plain old fashioned intuition. But let me tell you, she thinks her butt weighs a ton!"

Africa laughed, looked again at the picture, and with a pounding heart replaced it in the drawer. With her arms full of soiled linens, she darted out the door.

Bam! There was an irresistible force, and when she saw who it was, she all but fainted.

"Oh! Oh!", was all she could say.

This time two stooped to pick up the results of their collision. Sheets, towels, and linens seemed to be everywhere.

The young man smiled, his deep set eyes twinkled. Once again, she was facing the object of her many dreams.

"You don't curse on Mondays?" he teased.

Struggling for composure, and again holding an arm full of linens, Africa smiled and quickly dropped her bundle into the hamper just outside the door.

"Too close to Sunday," she retorted.

"What's going on out there?" called Mrs. Hildenbrandt from behind her flowered screen.

Together the young people entered the room. Africa stood at the foot of the bed, while the young man went to Mrs. Hildenbrandt, and kissed her affectionately on the cheek.

"Just got back into town, Grandma, and I couldn't wait to see you."

"Don't hand me that, Kevin. Sounds like the two of you have already met," she said, taking note of Africa.

"No, not really", said Africa, with a coy smile.

"Well, now, Kevin, this is my very special nurse, Miss Africa Jones. Meet my grandson, Dr. Kevin Hildenbrandt."

Once again Africa was surprised, and her hand trembled slightly as she extended it to him.

Doctor, she thought. She felt awed. Quickly, she recalled that there were times when Mrs. Hildenbrandt mentioned her grandson, the physician.

Their touch was electrifying, but to her surprise, once her smaller, delicate hand was in his, and his strong fingers closed about hers, she felt a warm, comfortable feeling. It was as if her hand now fit into a glove, which it had been seeking, and where it belonged. Although her heart continued to pound, she felt a calmness slowly creep over her. Their eyes met, and for seconds they were again lost in one another. Mrs. Hildenbrandt cleared her throat. The two released each others hand as they turned to face her. She wore a smile on her fine looking face.

"Africa, it's dinner time for you isn't it?"

"Yes, Mam."

"All right then, Kevin. Take her down to that chicken place on the corner. I know you just got here, but we can talk later."

Africa started to speak, but Mrs. Hildenbrandt interrupted her.

"Quiet now, Child. You know you've only got those cold sandwiches Lucy makes." She quickly turned her attention to Kevin.

"Kevin, get the show on the road!"

Africa's bright eyes glowed when she turned to Kevin. He smiled down at her in triumph.

"Let's go", he said, leading her to the door.

Africa never did get the chicken. As a matter of fact, she didn't get any dinner at all. Upon her return to New Hope, she was too happy and excited to even eat Lucy's lunch, which Mrs. Hildenbrandt had referred to earlier.

After she had clocked out for lunch, she and Kevin went to his new SL Mercedes, which was parked in the hospital's parking lot. This was located on the building's east side, where windows for the stucco structure were obstructed by a high wall, which was constructed to keep out burglars and make a tiny patio for each room.

"How much lunch time do they give a pretty nurse."

"I wouldn't know. I'm really not a nurse, not yet."

"No? What about all those books you carry."

"I'm a student nurse at Cal State and I work here as a Nurses' Aide."

Well, they're indeed fortunate. Now, how much time does a pretty Nurses' Aide rate?"

"One half hour", she said smiling at him. "And I figure we've only got about twenty-three minutes left." They were seated in the car.

He leaned closer in the darkness. She caught the masculine scent of his after shave lotion. His nearness again brought forth a pleasant excitement, and she felt her heart beats accelerating. Their lips met, and the softness and gentleness of his kiss was almost unbelievable in its sweetness. There were long moments before he released her. She surprised herself reaching for his mouth again with her own and slipping her arms about his neck. Again they kissed, and this time when he released her she felt a beautiful weakness. His lips caressed her ear lobes, her cheeks, and her eyes.

"I can't believe this. You are so beautiful", he whispered between kisses.

Africa felt completely lost in the overwhelming passion of his kisses.

"This can't be real", she whispered. "It's like we're under some sort of a spell", she managed.

"Witchcraft, I'm converted", murmured Kevin.

After a few more long, soul touching kisses, Kevin seemed to abruptly tear himself from her. He leaned back in his seat, and sighed deeply. Africa understood that their session must end, and she did not reach for him.

Kevin turned on the dashboard lights, and checked his watch.

"I'm sorry, Sweetheart, but I'm afraid we just lost your lunch period. You're got only three more minutes."

Africa laughed.

"Are you serious? We haven't been here that long, or have we?"

"We have, and I've enjoyed every precious minute", said Kevin.

"But, we never got out of the parking lot", she said. They both laughed, and again he held her.

"Can I take you to dinner tomorrow?" he asked.

Africa worked the next evening, and it so happened that Kevin was on call at the County Hospital on her next night off. Finally they set a date for the following Saturday night.

After hastily making arrangements, they kissed one long, passionate kiss, after which Kevin whispered in her ear, "I don't know how I'm going to wait until Saturday for another."

Me either," she answered breathlessly.

He helped her out of the car, then held her close to him for a moment. It seemed that she tore herself away when they parted. She ran from the parking lot, and to work. Turning, at the side of the building, she felt secure as she saw his figure standing in the semi darkness, watching for her.

Later that evening, while doing her final charting at the nurses' station, a delivery man appeared, asking for her. He had two boxes. One contained a dozen beautiful, red roses, and the other a gourmet, chicken dinner.

No one, she thought, had ever given her flowers in her whole life, with the exception of Billy. Occasionally, when he was a little boy, he would thrust a simple bouquet into her hands that he had plucked from backyard gardens. He did this to express his love for her. Africa was on cloud nine for the remainder of her shift. Even Billy was surprised at her exhilaration when they walked home later that night.

Lucy called her usual greeting, but declined Africa's invitation to join them in the kitchen for a snack. Together Billy and Africa sat at the kitchen table, and enjoyed the dinner which had born a loving note from Kevin. Africa kept the note hidden in her purse and when Billy asked who gave her the beautiful roses, and the delicious dinner, she replied,

"The family of one of my patients."

Africa wasn't hungry, and only partook a small portion of the dinner. She watched happily, her bright eyes dreamy, as Billy devoured the feast.

"Look, Sis," he said, washing his food down with gulps of soda, "All I got to say is, please keep in good with that family."

"I plan to," she responded with a smile.

CHAPTER 4

he weekend couldn't come too quickly for Africa. Classmates, patients and co-workers complimented her new glow. Early mornings she hummed or sang a catchy tune, while preparing to leave for her long day. Lucy couldn't figure it out except that her daughter was really falling for Chuck Wilson, and didn't want to say so. Africa had always been a pleasant child, but now she was joyous. One night, on the way home, she divided her books between herself and Billy, then challenged him to a race. He declined, shouting,

"Hey, cool it, Sis! I don't like running with this iron!"

Mrs. Hildenbrandt chuckled when Africa told her that she and Kevin had chatted in his car. She too, noticed Africa's new zest and radiance. The girl's dark eyes were brighter than ever, when she told Mrs. Hildenbrandt about their forthcoming Saturday night date.

"You seem to like him very much, Africa. You just met."

"I know. It's fantastic, but I can't bother to try and figure it out. Tell me about Kevin, Mrs. Hildenbrandt. I want to know all about him.

"I've told you a lot about Kevin. Don't you remember? I'm the old one, and I remember telling you lots of things."

"But I didn't know him then! Please. I just want to hear it all over again, and more."

"No way. I'll leave that to him. I don't plan to get involved in any mess. You two can do your own thing." That was all Africa could manage to get out of her friend.

There was only one problem that disturbed Africa. That was Chuck Wilson. Twice he had met her when she came on duty, and asked for a date. He knew that she was off on Saturday, and made that evening his choice. The first time she was able to put him off with, "I'll see," while she tried to think up a good reason. But this second time, when he insisted on the following Saturday night, she just had to tell him that she had made other plans. He became angry, and almost knocked the time clock off the wall, when she would not reconsider. Fortunately, another nurse appeared, so he walked toward his office in a huff. If Africa didn't know it before, she knew now, that cooling Chuck Wilson was going to be a problem.

On Saturday morning, the day after payday, Africa did something very unusual. She returned from the bank, after cashing her check. Lucy was ironing in the kitchen, when she gave her the envelope containing all her pay. This was her custom.

"Mom, can you possibly hold out on something this pay day? I need about sixty dollars. I'll ask for extra time next weekend to make up for it."

"Africa, I'm surprised. What do you need sixty for? You never ask for anything."

"I know, Mom, but this is special. I've got a date this evening, and I saw a dress on sale that I'd like to buy. It's important, Mom, I really would like to look great!"

"Honey, you know this is your money. You pay most of the bills around here anyway. I always tell you to take out a little somethin' for yourself. Of course you take sixty! I don't know what not to pay, but I'll come up with somethin'."

"Mom, I feel real guilty."

Lucy set the iron in it's case and put her arms about her daughter.

"Don't, Honey. Please don't. You're a good girl and you deserve somethin' nice once in awhile. I want you to look pretty when you go out with Chuck Wilson, too."

Africa was quiet. Lucy counted out sixty dollars to her daughter, then kissed her on the check. She stuffed the envelope in her bosom.

"That no good Moses will probably be hanging around here today. I don't trust him worth a damn. Been job hunting now for almost two years. Brenda's welfare check will probably be in the mail today, too. You can pay the utilities Monday. That's your early day home from school, isn't it?"

"Yes, Mom," said Africa in a flat tone.

"Mr. Carter is pretty nice. He can wait another two weeks for the rest of his plumbing bill. Just hope nothing else breaks down in the meantime."

Africa looked at her mother with concern.

"What's wrong, Baby?"

"Mom, my date is not Chuck Wilson. I told you I would never go out with him again."

"What? Nobody else is worth sixty dollars, Africa! Now I got one mess around here, and I don't plan to have another. Who is it? Give me that money."

Lucy had again stopped ironing, and was holding out her hand.

"Mom, please!" Africa turned to leave the room.

"Africa!"

"Mom, it's Mrs. Hildenbrandt's grandson. His name is Kevin, and he's a doctor."

"What? Child, what you say? The Mrs. Hildenbrandt?"

Africa nodded in the affirmative.

"Go on, get you a dress. You think you need some more?" Lucy said as she reached to her bosom.

Africa laughed and ran from the room. "No, Mom. No."

She could hear Lucy laughing and saying "Whoeee!"

That evening when Kevin arrived to pick up Africa for their date, everybody was home, even the neighborhood gang took time out from playing baseball in the street to admire the new Mercedes. Moses whom Lucy wouldn't let in the house until he had a job, was sitting on the front steps with Brenda and Joey. Lucy was furious when she heard Brenda

48

introduce Joey, and then Moses as her boyfriend. Moses extended his hand with a

"Hey, Doc! Glad to meet ya."

Africa opened the door as he was beginning to tell Kevin about his sinusitis.

Africa delighted in the hospitable and gracious manner in which Lucy greeted Kevin. She smiled, extended her hand, and spoke her most proper English.

"It is indeed a pleasure, Dr. Hildenbrandt," she said.

Kevin and Billy talked football for a few minutes, until Lucy's scowl silenced her son's animated remarks. Kevin had revealed his college football career, and both Lucy and Africa knew the conversation could continue for hours.

Africa was lovelier than ever. Her new, silk dress was an eggshell blue, and was a striking compliment to her smooth, brown complexion, and dark hair. It molded perfectly to her body, and a ribbon sash was drawn daintily about her slender waist. The fully pleated skirt came just below her knees, and swirled each time she turned to reveal pretty knees, and well proportioned legs, set off by high heeled, beige sandals. A low cut neckline revealed the voluptuous swelling of her breasts. She wore a single gold chain from which dangled a delicate, baroque pearl. This was a cherished gift from her family last Christmas. She was pleased with her appearance, and knew from Kevin's smiling eyes that he was too. Lucy was amazed that such a dress could be purchased so cheaply. Africa had explained to her, earlier, that the dress was a small sized sample, which had been saved for her by a friendly saleslady.

Just before Kevin arrived there had been quite a discussion as to what type wrap she should carry. Her dress had only short, caplet sleeves, and the evenings were still cool. Brenda had insisted she wear the short mink stole that Moses had given her when Joey was born. Lucy was dubious. Billy swore that Moses had bought it hot, and he didn't want his sister picked up for wearing hot goods. Brenda didn't deny this, but said nobody would be examining the jacket. It indeed looked fantastic on Africa, rich and luxurious. No model could have worn it better. Africa finally decided she would use it.

"O.K.! O.K.! But don't let a cop stop you, they might decide to check it out," shouted Billy.

"Throw it out the window, if they do," suggested Lucy.

"Like hell!" screamed Brenda, reaching for her jacket.

Africa was as much impressed with Kevin as he was with her. He was suave, cool and handsome in his navy blue suit, and red silk tie. Just looking at him gave her goose pimples. For the first time in her life, she could hardly think of anything to say. At times, she found herself just looking at him. She hoped he didn't think she was stupid.

Kevin maneuvered his luxury, sports car with expertise in and out of traffic. The rainy season had gone, leaving everything fresh and green. Africa was enjoying the ride immensely. Neither had much to say, at first. They just exchanged highly charged glances, and satisfied smiles.

"O.K., My Lady, where would you like to go?"

"Whatever suits you is all right with me," Africa answered sweetly.

"Well, I've got tickets for a play at the Music Center. How's about dinner and then a play?"

"Great! I'd love it!" Africa was excited.

"We're on our way," said Kevin as he turned a quick corner.

"Do the police bother you much with this fantastic car, Kevin?"

"No, I haven't had any trouble. You don't like my driving?"

"No, no, I think you're a wonderful driver. I just don't want the police to stop us tonight."

"Me either, but why not tonight?"

"Well, this jacket I'm wearing, ah, ah,," Africa hesitated.

"It's beautiful, just like the girl inside it," said Kevin, giving her an admiring glance.

"Thank you, but I, ah, well, I think it's hot!"

After she said it, Africa felt she shouldn't have. Kevin looked at her, his deep eyes serious, then he laughed earnestly, bending slightly over the steering wheel.

"O.K.," he said finally, "You can bet, I'll be extra careful!"

Just before turning onto the freeway entrance, Kevin pulled to the side of the street, and stopped the engine. He looked at Africa, a softness in her eyes seemed to devour her. His hand reached for a lock of her soft, wavy hair.

"Sweetheart, I just had to tell you that you're the most beautiful thing I've ever seen."

"You really think so?" managed Africa. She was never conscious of her true beauty.

"I know so," he whispered as he kissed her tenderly.

"That was worth waiting all week for," he said, putting the lock of hair back into place. They looked at each other for a long moment and then kissed again. This time Africa's hand fell into place behind his neck. He lifted his mouth from hers and smiled.

"We are going to the theater. No parking lot scene tonight!"

Africa laughed happily as Kevin started the engine, then drove onto the freeway.

Both enjoyed their dinner in the center's plush dining room. The service was as excellent as the food. While eating, they exchanged interesting information about each other. Africa learned that Kevin's father, Mrs. Hildenbrandt's only son, was also a physician. Kevin was thirty-one years old and had an older brother, who, after finishing college had taken over as president of the insurance company which their grandfather, Mr. Hildenbrandt, had founded. The brother's wife, Jeannie, came from a socially prominent family. Africa recognized her maiden name. Kevin was in his last year's residency at County Hospital, and in July, he would become a full fledged, Board Certified Surgeon.

Africa told Kevin about Billy being first up for winning a four year football scholarship to college in September, and Lucy's illness which developed after the death of her father. He asked about Moses and Brenda. Africa quite candidly filled him in on all the details, mainly Joey.

"I hope he finds a job," finished Africa, with a sigh. "Oh, incidentally, Moses is responsible for the mink jacket. It's Brenda's. Billy swears it's hot."

Kevin was as fascinated by her frankness as he was concerning everything else about Africa.

Later, in the darkened theater they held hands. Africa swore to herself that she felt electricity enter her body from Kevin's through their entwined hands. The play was a musical-comedy with a mixed black and white cast. Both Kevin and Africa's laughter was genuine and refreshing. At intermission, they sipped champagne. Africa informed Kevin that champagne was all she could drink, and that two was her limit.

After the theater, both felt the night was too young to end, so Kevin drove quickly to Hollywood. They spent an exciting hour in a crowded, rocking bistro. Africa drank her second glass of champagne, and then started on cola with a lemon twist. The music was too loud for talking, and too swinging for sitting, so they danced the night away, laughing and having the time of their lives. Africa was shocked to find Kevin such an expert dancer. He was cool and moved with the ease of a natural born dancer. Africa was a pleasure to watch. She loved to dance, and

Kevin didn't make a move that she couldn't follow. With her bright eyes flashing, her skin aglow, and skirt swirling about her lovely legs, Africa was a sight to behold, as she and Kevin cleared space on the crowded dance floor. Her laughter sometimes outdid the combo.

When they kissed goodnight at her door, it was two in the morning. Both agreed this had been one of the most exciting evenings of their lives. Kevin had to be in surgery at eight in the morning, and was on call all day Sunday, but he agreed to call her. Africa didn't leave the house until he called at four the next afternoon. He only had a few minutes, but in those they agreed that they missed each other terribly, and could hardly wait for their next date, which would take place the following weekend.

It was good that Africa enjoyed the weekend, because Monday she would have to draw on that happiness for strength. She was totally unprepared for the new turn of events that awaited her.

CHAPTER 5

s usual Africa rushed to work at New Hope. It had been a good day for her at school. She had passed her exams in Pediatrics with an "A". Everything's going my way she thought as she stopped at the time clock. There was a note attached to her time card. Opening it she read, "After this shift, your services are terminated at New Hope. Please come to the Director of Nurses' office for your final check".

Africa could hardly believe what she had read. She immediately felt weak. The thought of being without her job was terrifying. Her family needed her salary, and she needed it to finish college. What had she done? There must be some mistake, she thought.

Miss Thornton was sitting at her desk, when Africa appeared at her office door.

"I've been expecting you", she told the girl, holding out an envelope which Africa knew must be her severance pay.

"Why, Miss Thonton? What have I done?" she asked in dismay.

"Well, for one thing, you've been late three times this past month."

"But never more that five or six minutes, Miss Thornton. You remember, I told you how the buses run slow sometimes, and I transfer three times to get here."

"That's your problem, not mine. You're supposed to be here on time and you're not. Secondly, I don't approve of women who court their boyfriends on the premises, and on their employer's time," said Miss Thornton in a contemptuous tone.

It was then that Africa understood. Someone had seen her and Kevin kissing that night in the parking lot, and told. Miss Thornton knew everything that ever happened in and within the vicinity of New Hope. There was always someone willing to offer information in expectation of brownie points.

Without another word, she took the envelope with her paycheck, and left the office. She would not give this nasty woman the pleasure of seeing her beg.

After the secretary announced Africa, she was admitted into Chuck Wilson's comfortable office. It was so large and plush that it did not seem to be a part of the rest of the hospital. Chuck kept his seat behind his big, mahogany desk, but offered Africa a seat, which she ignored.

"Chuck, Miss Thornton just fired me. She gave me this check. You must know about this. What's going on?"

Chuck smiled. "Yeah, I know. She's been after you a long time, Africa."

"Well, why did you let her do it? You know this job is very important to me, and my whole family. I need my job, Chuck!"

He looked very serious and Africa detected a note of anger in his voice. "Who's the clown you've been making out with lately? I heard about that parking lot episode. I don't guess you're a virgin any more since your Saturday night date."

"That, Mr. Wilson, is really none of your business. I'm here about my job, not my personal life!" Africa felt herself becoming angry.

"I'm making it my business, Baby!" retorted Chuck.

Africa glared at him, her bright eyes larger and very intense. She turned to leave. Chuck was up and out from behind the desk in an instant. He grabbed Africa by the shoulders.

"Look, Baby. One word from you and you've got your job and more. Miss Thornton will go tomorrow. I'll bring in another director until you graduate, get your license, and learn the ropes, then it's yours, all yours. And if you don't want that, just plan to stay at home and look pretty, have my kids, and have fun. We'll go to Europe for our honeymoon, a whole month. Just say yes, Africa. Say you'll marry me!"

Africa stared at Chuck. The both of them could feel her anger cool. In spite of all that was happening to her, she felt sorry for him. She spoke quietly but with conviction.

"Chuck, I'm not for sale."

"What's your family going to say about your losing your job?"

"I can tell you this much, Chuck. They wouldn't want me to sell myself either."

"Don't be too sure," he said pulling her to him and crushing her mouth with his. She struggled out of his embrace, slapped him hard, and ran from the office.

59

"Africa Jones, you'll regret this! I'll remember it all when you come crawling back for your job," he hissed after her.

When Mrs. Hildenbrandt saw Africa's face, she knew trouble was in the brew. Africa told her all of what had happened. When she finished, the old lady was silent with thought. Africa began to cry.

"Hush, Child! You've done fine so far, now don't mess up. You don't have to crawl for nobody. I've seen this coming for a long time. Now, don't you worry I've got plans. Go home now, rest yourself, and I'll call you later."

"Yes Mam," answered Africa. She trusted Mrs. Hildenbrandt, and felt assured she would place enough pressure on someone to get her job back.

When Africa reached home, the family was having dinner at the kitchen table. Africa told them what had happened. There was much excitement, everyone forgetting dinner and trying to talk at once.

"Africa, marry him. I wish I had that chance or he was Moses. What's wrong with you?" Brenda finally yelled in desperation. Joey had begun to cry, and she commenced hushing and rocking him in her lap.

"Don't be no fool, Girl!" shouted Lucy. "Up to now, you've always had pretty good sense.

60

You've got a chance to put yourself on easy street, now take it!"

"No you don't, Africa," yelled Billy. "You told him you're not for sale, and you're damned right. I'll quit school first. Forget college!" Little did he know, but his statement would have more influence than any of the others towards having her change of mind. She definitely did not want her Billy to drop out of school.

After the family's traumatic input, Africa went into the bedroom she shared with Brenda and Joey. She stretched out on the bed and stared at the ceiling, and was just about to drift off to sleep, when Lucy came in and sat on the side of the bed.

"Africa, Honey, I just want what's best for you. I always have favored Chuck Wilson. Mrs. Hildenbrandt's grandson might be fine, he's a doctor and all, but we don't know what he might do, and a bird in the hand is worth two in the bush."

"Mom, how can you say these things to me? Didn't you love Daddy? Would you have thought of getting married to someone else when you were in love with Daddy? Would you have married someone you didn't love just for money?"

"Africa, I'm going to tell you something. I've had years to think, and learn. You're like me starting all over again. I was very much in love with

61

a young man when I was your age. He didn't have a job, worked awhile here and there and quit. Said he couldn't stand being tied down. Well, when I became pregnant he just up and left town, disappeared."

"Mom!"

"Brenda was three months old when your father married me. He loved me. I wasn't really in love with him. What I felt before, I've never felt again. But I learned to love your father, and although I worked and we didn't have an awful lot, we had a good life. You know that. He took good care of us all and because of him, we've got a roof over our heads now. You can learn to love a man who is good to you, and Chuck Wilson, would be good to you. I know it, Child." She finished by gently caressing her daughter's hand.

Africa looked at her mother in shocked silence.

"Mom, I can't get over it. Brenda and I are not whole sisters?"

"No. That's why she looks so different from you and Billy. Her father was very fair skinned, almost white. That's why she turned out so light. Leroy adopted her as his own, and people probably think she took from back in the family. Brenda knows. I told her when she got mixed up with

62

Moses, hoping it would help her to get rid of him, instead she got pregnant with Joey.

"Brenda knows! Does Billy know?" asked Africa.

"No. I haven't found any reason to tell him, yet."

"Oh, Mom. I'm so sorry. You really had a bad time," said Africa, as she sat up and embraced her mother. "You never heard from Brenda's real father again?"

"No, but about six years after Leroy and I were married, I heard he had gotten mixed up with some gangsters in Chicago, and was killed. He always said he was going to make the big time, even if it killed him, and I guess it did."

After her mother left, Africa was deep in thought. She had not made up her mind as to what she should do next. Should she look for another job, or take off from school for awhile? There was one thing, however, that she knew that she could not do, and that was to marry Chuck Wilson. She finally decided to just wait and see if Mrs. Hildenbrandt could get back her job.

It was after nine o'clock when the phone rang. Africa was studying at the kitchen table. It was Kevin. She was so happy to hear his voice.

"Look, Sweetheart," he said in his deep, warm, masculine voice. "I heard the news, but I'm not calling it bad. I just don't want you to worry. Grandma's working on something great, and everything is going to be all right."

He told her that he had talked to Mrs. Hildenbrandt just a little while earlier, that she called him at the hospital. He wouldn't reveal to Africa what was in the making, because he said he wanted to give his grandmother the pleasure of telling her since it was all her idea. He asked her to please go to New Hope the next afternoon, just as she always did, but to see his grandmother before she spoke to anyone. Africa agreed. That night she slept well because, she had been so overjoyed to hear from Kevin and trusted him and Mrs. Hildenbrandt to help her.

CHAPTER 6

he next afternoon, Africa alighted from the bus as usual, however, this time she did not rush as she walked towards the New Hope Convalescent Hospital. It seemed incredible that she wasn't going to work, or was she? Well, the last she had heard was that she was fired, and no one had contacted her to the contrary. What could Mrs. Hildenbrandt do? Maybe she could get her job back for her. The woman was influential and Chuck listed her as a VIP She had overheard him say that she was the longest and best paying private patient that New Hope ever had. He insisted she should have the very best service.

Perhaps Mrs. Hildenbrandt did get her job back for her. If that should be the case, it was best she not be any more late than usual, thought Africa.

She quickened her pace, and in spite of her heavy arm load of books, she ran up the steps to enter the hospital. Inside she met several co-workers, who stopped to verify the fact that she had been fired. Quite candidly, she confirmed the rumor, and proceeded to Mrs. Hildenbrandt's room. She saw Miss Thornton pass stiffly in the corridor ahead of her. The woman gave her a mean scowl. Wow, what's gone down? thought Africa. That look meant something has happened that didn't please her one bit, and if that's the case it must be good for me, were her continued thoughts.

When Africa entered Mrs. Hildenbrandt's room, she was surprised to find boxes and suitcases all over the place. The old lady smiled and greeted her warmly.

"Well dear, come on in! We've lots of work to do here."

"Mrs. Hildenbrandt, what's going on? All these suitcases and everything! Are you going somewhere?"

"Indeed I am. I'm going home and I want you to go with me."

"I don't think I understand," said Africa bewildered.

Mrs. Hildenbrandt motioned to the comfortable arm chair at her bedside.

66

"Take a seat, dear. Put down those heavy books. I've got something to tell you."

After Africa was seated, she began.

"I don't like what's happened to you here, Africa. I didn't even ask them to rehire you. I've decided to go home. I've got a lovely, big home. The whole family lives there. My son and his wife, who is a pain. They're Kevin and Mark's parents. Mark is carrying on the family insurance business that my husband started. He's married to another pain, and that's why I came here in the first place, just to get away from it all. I turned the house over to them all. Kevin lives there too, when he's not at the hospital. He's my heart, Africa. I want you to know that, my dear. He's always been so thoughtful and good to me."

She paused for a moment, then took a deep breath as she continued.

"I'm confined to my bed anyway, so I couldn't see any difference in being here or there. At least here, I felt I would have some peace."

Africa smiled, and Mrs. Hildenbrandt squeezed her hand.

"Now here's the deal," whispered the old lady, and her eyes twinkled, "I had a very frank talk with Dr. Anderson last night. I called him over here. Just as I suspected, this cancer is acting up again,

67

and I'm not going to last much longer. I would rather die in my own home, Child. So he discharged me. But you have to go home with me. I really need you. With you, I can stand it there. You'll get paid more than you do here, a considerable amount more."

Africa started to speak, "I don't drive, and.."

Mrs. Hildenbrandt interrupted, "Don't worry about that. You can learn, and until you do, I'll make arrangements."

"Oh, Mrs. Hildenbrandt! For real?" asked Africa. She was overcome with what she was hearing.

"Of course, and I've got answers to all your questions, Child. I know you're still in school, and I want you to stay there. If the good Lord will spare me, I just might be around for your graduation.

Africa gave Mrs. Hildenbrandt an encouraging smile, as she said, "Of course you will, and for a long time afterward. You only have to believe it!"

"I've never been one to kid myself, Africa. Now I plan for you to keep your same schedule. My home is a little ways from the bus line, so I'm going to let you use my car."

Africa interrupted her, "Mrs. Hildenbrandt , I don't dr.."

It was now Mrs. Hildenbrandt's turn to interrupt.

"I told you I'd take care of that. You don't think I'm crazy, now. I know exactly what I'm doing. Now you just listen. My car, it's a seven year old Cadillac, been in the garage ever since I've been here, but Jose has kept it in good shape. Lupe will take care of my needs in the morning and I'll look for you in the afternoon."

Africa had met Jose and Lupe Garcia. They had worked as Mrs. Hildenbrandt's handyman and housekeeper for twenty years, and lived in quarters back of the kitchen.

"You can have any two days, a week, you choose to be off," continued Mrs. Hildenbrandt. "That might help with your school schedule; give you time off, for study, before an exam, maybe."

Africa became more and more elated as she listened to Mrs. Hildenbrandt.

"Now, you'll have to sleep over."

"I don't mind at all. Oh, thank you, Mrs. Hildenbrandt. It all sounds too good to be true!"

"Well, it's true all right. Now get yourself busy and let's pack up my things. The ambulance will be here to pick us up at six. We haven't got much time."

"You've forgotten one thing, Mrs. Hildenbrandt. I don't drive."

"I never forget anything, and you know it," scolded the old lady. "You can learn to drive and in the meantime, I'll make arrangements."

Africa laughed with excitement and happiness, as she turned her attention to Mrs. Hildenbrandt's baggage.

"All this won't fit in the ambulance, Mrs. Hildenbrandt," remarked Africa, as she surveyed the room and closets.

"I know, I know, Child. I thought this thing out months ago, but I didn't want to leave without you, and I didn't think Mr. Wilson would put you on loan. Well, he and old battle-ax have played right into my hands."

"I heard that," said Africa, as she sprung into action, both laughed as Africa began packing. Mrs. Hildenbrandt cheerfully directed, looking like a grand old queen, in her satin and lace.

"Jose will be here with a truck tomorrow, and pick up all this junk you pack, and any book shelves, and books.

Africa heard Mrs. Hildenbrandt sigh, and ask, "Well what do you want?"

Turning, she found Chuck Wilson standing in the doorway. She had been so busy, she had not heard him open the door. He walked closer to Mrs. Hildenbrandt and his face was without his usual smile. He always wore a smile when he entered Mrs. Hildenbrandt's room. He looked sad, and avoided Africa's eyes.

"Hi, Africa," he said. She detected a hint of remorse in his tone. She coolly returned his greeting.

"Good afternoon, Mr. Wilson."

He asked Mrs. Hildenbrandt if she wouldn't reconsider, and stay on, whereupon, she lit into him like a fire cracker, telling him how he should be ashamed of the way he treated Africa, and permitted his head nurse to do likewise. Africa had paused momentarily in her packing, just in case Mrs. Hildenbrandt changed her mind.

"Move it, Child!" she commanded. "There's not a chance I'd stay here another night. Let's get this show on the road!" she said to Africa, turning away from Chuck as if he were no longer present. When he entered the room, he was depressed, but when he left, he was thoroughly beaten.

It was barely two hours later that the ambulance paused at the iron gate occluding Mrs. Hildenbrandt's driveway. The driver spoke into a little microphone, built into the entrails of the gate, whereupon it parted, and the ambulance entered.

71

Africa was totally unprepared for the sight before her eyes. The Hildenbrandt home was more beautiful than she would have dared imagine. It sat behind a curved driveway, which encased a magnificently manicured lawn, bordered with tropical plants and flowers of all hues. The house was two stories, of pink stucco, with white trimming that reminded her of icing on a birthday cake. The roof was covered with an odd, rolled type gray shingles, and she instantly thought of the houses she used to see in her book of fairy tales. The whole scene, house and grounds, was magnificent in its beauty, and enhanced by the late afternoon sunlight.

Mrs. Hildenbrandt watched Africa's expression as she asked her, "You like it?"

"I can't believe it," answered Africa.

No one was at home but the hired couple, Lupe and Jose Garcia. Africa remembered Jose from the times when he brought books to the hospital or ran errands for Mrs. Hildenbrandt. He was a tall, thin man with a mustache, whom she could easily visualize in a sombrero, and dressed as a fine Spanish gentleman. His wife, Lupe, was short and plump. She wore a thick, black braid which rested on her ample hips, and a warm friendly smile. Africa knew Kevin was on call at the hospital and couldn't get away, but she wondered about the rest of the family.

Once inside, she was again stunned. Never before had she seen such luxurious elegance. There were marble floors, rich, colorful oriental carpeting, crystal chandeliers, and fine mahogany furniture, polished to perfection. She followed the ambulance attendants as they carried Mrs. Hildenbrandt's stretcher up the artistically and beautifully curved staircase, then down a richly carpeted hallway, decorated with exquisite paintings, and into her rooms.

They passed through a quaint and cheerful ante-room into Mrs. Hildenbrandt's bedroom, which was large with high ceilings, French windows, and a lovely, old English fireplace. The covers were drawn back on a magnificent, four posted, canopied bed, in anticipation of a queen's arrival.

This is how Africa perceived Mrs. Hildenbrandt when she looked at her in the Old English setting of her room. Africa learned that the ante-room through which they had just passed served as Mrs. Hildenbrandt's sitting room, and it was to be her quarters. The room was lovely. It also contained a fireplace, and it was decorated in a beautiful shade of azure blue with handsome, mahogany furnishings with velvet upholstery. The deep piled carpeting was soft, rich and blue. A large sofa, when pulled out, would serve as a comfortable bed for her. Both rooms contained private baths, large and well appointed with marble and gold plated fixtures. Mrs. Hildenbrandt told Africa, that the antique desk, with exquisite carving and design, would be hers for study. Africa loved it all. She estimated that her whole house would fit into just Mrs. Hildenbrandt's suite alone. It all so fascinated her that she was speechless for a time. Mrs. Hildenbrandt remarked about her being so quiet. When she recovered all she could say was that everything was just so beautiful that she didn't know what to say. It never occurred to her that Mrs. Hildenbrandt could have such wealth. If the rest of the house was like this, then she was indeed in heaven.

Africa called Lucy to tell her all that had transpired, and that she would not be home until the following evening after school.

"Tell Billy not to meet me tonight, Mom. I'll be spending the night here. Mom, it is out of sight! I can't even describe how beautiful it is here. All I can say is that it is out of sight!"

"Well, I wouldn't expect it to be different. Everybody knows how rich the Hildenbrandts are.

Don't you get into nothing up there! What you gonna sleep in?"

"It's all taken care of, Mom. Mrs. Hildenbrandt has given me a gorgeous gown, and robe to match. It was hers, years ago. She's got everything here, right down to a supply of new tooth brushes. She even made arrangements for the uniform and things I have on to be laundered tonight, shoes polished too, and ready for me to wear to school in the morning. Jose, her handyman, will drive me there and pick me up. Can you beat that! And I'm going to make more money to boot!"

"Praise the Lord. But Africa, is that man gonna drive you every day?"

"No, Mom. Mrs. Hildenbrandt's loaned me her Cadillac, and soon as I get my driver's license, I'll be on wheels!"

"Say what? You don't mean it!" exclaimed Lucy.

"Now don't worry. I'm fine, Mom and there's nothing for me to get into 'cepting the bed."

"Well, you just make sure you're in it by yourself. There ain't no telling what goes on in these rich folks houses."

"Oh, Mom!" chided Africa.

"Well , I ain't for no mess, but it's a good thing, I pretty much trust Mrs. Hildenbrandt," Lucy conceded.

Later that evening, Mrs. Hildenbrandt and Africa enjoyed a delicious dinner prepared by Lupe. Africa was seated at a small round table, in front of the large bay windows, which overlooked a garden, beautiful with palm trees, and a variety of colorful plants. The pool area, with a bubbling Jacuzzi and the spacious tennis court, all seemed too beautiful to be real. Africa wondered momentarily if she just might be enjoying a fantastic painting, and then she saw Jose walking through the painting towards the house, and she knew it was all very real.

Mrs. Hildenbrandt's bed was one which could be adjusted to several comfortable positions. She now sat upright, lifting silver lids and examining all the delectable surprises Lupe had made for them.

"I didn't know a Mexican cook could prepare such tasty soul food. These greens and yams taste just like my mom's," said Africa.

Mrs. Hildenbrandt gave her special chuckle, as she confided to Africa, "When Lupe and Jose started here with me, mind you, twenty-five years ago, that was the first thing I taught Lupe. My husband said he couldn't live on Mexican food

76

every day. I think I taught her pretty good. We've got the best of two worlds here, when it comes to dining."

"I can attest to that ," said a familiar voice from the doorway."

It was Kevin, dressed in a green scrub suit under a white coat. Both Mrs. Hildenbrandt and Africa cried his name as he entered the room.

"Welcome home, Grandma," he said, giving her a kiss on the cheek. Turning to Africa, he grasped the hand she extended to him, and kissed it ever so gently while searching her eyes.

"For the most beautiful girl in the world," he said softly. "Thank you," said Africa, with a demure but tempting smile.

"Sit down there, Kevin, next to Africa. I'll bet you haven't had dinner." Mrs. Hildenbrandt then pulled a gold, velvet cord, which hung from the canopy of her bed, and chimes sounded throughout the house.

"No, come to think of it, I haven't" replied Kevin. "But, I'll have to rush. I have exactly one hour. I got a buddy to fill in for me. No way could I not welcome you home, Grandma. This is quite an occasion, and it gives me a chance to see Africa too." He finished while seating his magnificent, masculine body into a Queen Anne chair at the table. It was good that Africa had eaten most of her meal before his arrival, because now, Kevin's virile presence quelled her appetite. Just looking at him, another appetite, of whose existence she had not been aware, was growing and gnawing within her. The excitement was tense, but delightful.

This fascination I have for him has to be love, she thought. Suddenly the realization hit her. Damn it, I do believe I've fallen in love, was the thought that screamed in her mind. In a way it was frightening. What's going to happen, was her concern. Love meant losing control of yourself, a powerlessness she feared. It meant being vulnerable to hurt, and taken for a fool. Be careful, keep your cool, she admonished herself.

Glancing at Kevin, her mind continued to work overtime. I wonder how he feels about me? Maybe he's just a flirt, and putting me on. Maybe his kisses were a means to an end. She sipped her coffee, and asked him if he had been very busy at the hospital. Lupe arrived while he was in the process of explaining his fifth surgery of the day, while attempting to also answer Africa and Mrs. Hildenbrandt's many questions. They were both delighted to see his avid interest in his work, and amazed at his wealth of knowledge.

After dinner, and his good-bye to Mrs. Hildenbrandt, Africa followed him to the door of the sitting room. He paused, slipped his arms about her, and held her close to him.

"See there, my love, didn't I tell you everything would work out just fine?"

"Yes, and I believed you. Thanks, because I was frantic before I talked with you." Her face was next to his and he whispered into her ear.

"Honey, I'm not sure what's going on with us, but I'm mad about you. I think about you all the time. It doesn't handicap me, really it's an inspiration.

He kissed her tenderly, first her eyes, her cheeks, and then her mouth, which returned his kiss with equal tenderness. They were locked tightly in a passionate embrace, when Mrs. Hildenbrandt's bedside chime seemed to shatter through to their ears.

"Good-bye for now," he whispered. "Don't forget our Saturday date. I'll meet you here?" he asked.

"Yes. Good-bye, Kevin."

Africa rushed back into the bedroom, with a feeling as high, as if she had drank from a magical potion. She took care of Mrs. Hildenbrandt's needs, by helping her on the bedpan. While in the bathroom, she leaned against the wall, and whispered to herself, "Oh! He is so fine!"

It was about twenty minutes after Kevin's departure, that Africa was preparing Mrs. Hildenbrandt for sleep, and hunting the old lady's face cream, which somehow had been misplaced. From the hallway floated laughter and a mixture of voices. Africa looked up to find several people entering the room. All were dressed in formal attire. Three of them she recognized. They were on the picture, which had been in Mrs. Hildenbrandt's drawer. Kevin's father, his mother, and the young woman, whom Mrs. Hildenbrandt identified as Kevin's girlfriend.

Africa had never mentioned the girl to Kevin, because she felt uncomfortable in the attempt. Several times she had tried, but just couldn't seem to find the right words. She felt that their involvement was not deep enough, and she did not wish to say anything to turn him off.

The entourage rushed around the bed, kissing and kidding Mrs. Hildenbrandt as they welcomed her home. Africa stood quietly by the bureau watching the scene. She suspected the young man to be Kevin's brother. He looked a great deal like Kevin but was darker in complexion. His coarse, black hair was wavy. The young woman, whom Africa suspected was his wife looked much like Kevin's mother, except for weight. She was olive complexion, blonde and somewhat plump. His mother was blonde, fair skinned and slender. Africa noted that the two women wore their hair in the same short, stylish bob. A reversal of body weight would have been more realistic, thought Africa, because of their ages. Kevin's father was of a rich, dark brown coloring, with beautiful, snow white hair. He was tall and handsome, and most definitely conveyed the Father image. Africa thought Kevin was a good cross between his parents, with his smooth, tan coloring, and his natural, dark brown hair. He obviously took his height, and broad shouldered, athletic build from his father. Africa studied the girlfriend. She was of a tan coloring, with wavy, light brown hair, which fell to her shoulders. Her face was pretty. She was not as tall as Africa, and had a nice figure. She seemed quite sure of herself with the family, laughing and talking with ease. She too, kissed Mrs. Hildenbrandt. Africa noticed the way she tossed her hair about as she talked. Her speech sounded exaggerated and affected, and every now and then she paused to toss her nose into the air. Africa concluded her to be a snob. She put Kevin's mother in the same category. All of them had noticed Africa standing quietly in the shadows, but only the men kept stealing glances in her direction.

"Africa come on over here," called Mrs. Hildenbrandt. "Come on, Child," she commanded, as Africa approached, somewhat hesitantly. "I want you folks to meet my nurse." Africa had not met them at New Hope. If they came, she thought, it was obviously seldom, and during the early afternoon.

"Miss Jones, meet my son, Dr. Hildenbrandt, and his wife, Mrs. Hildenbrandt, My grandson, Mark, and this is his wife, Jeannie, and our neighbor, Miss Nanette Lee." Africa was reassured that she had identified them correctly during her period of observation. She exchanged polite greetings with each of them. The men stared, as did Kevin's mother, but in a much more scrutinizing manner, while the two younger women proceeded to ignore her, and joined in a conversation amongst themselves.

"Africa will be living here as my nurse," explained the elder Mrs. Hildenbrandt.

"We're delighted to have you," said Dr. Hildenbrandt, "I might add," he continued, "you're the most beautiful nurse I've laid eyes on in a long, long time."

"I didn't realize they had such talent at New Hope," remarked Mark. The women immediately stopped conversing to direct disapproving glances at the men. Africa gave a demure smile as she responded, "Thank you. I'm flattered."

"I've always enjoyed beauty around me. You all know that," said Mrs. Hildenbrandt. "Now tell me, how was the play?" she asked.

"Fantastic! Terry was outstanding," said Dr. Hildenbrandt.

Listening to the conversation, Africa learned that they had attended a benefit performance for the Urban League. Nanette's sister, Terry, had a lead role in the play.

Mrs. Hildenbrandt finally dismissed them all, saying she was tired from a long, hard day, and that Africa had to get up early. This called for an explanation as to Africa's working hours, and her nursing studies at the state college.

"Working and trying to get a college degree must be horrendous," said Nanette. "I received my BA from Bennett, and my Masters from Columbia. Fortunately, I was able to devote my full time to study," she said. Her air was that of disdain, as she looked at Africa.

"It's not as bad as it sounds," said Africa. "I thank God for giving me the opportunity."

"That's the way I felt, Africa," said the elder Mrs. Hildenbrandt. "Mr. Hildenbrandt and I both did it the hard way."

"I'm impressed," said Dr. Hildenbrandt. We need more young people with your ambition."

"Anything impresses you," snapped his wife, as they left the room.

Before departing, Nanette squeezed the elder Mrs. Hildenbrandt's hand as she said, with delight, "Did Kevin tell you? We've set the date for our wedding. June fifteenth! Isn't that wonderful!"

Mrs. Hildenbrandt made no comment, except to say, "Really." Then she called, "Good night!" to the others already passing through the ante-room and in the hallway. She made a distasteful face, and waved her hand in Nanette's direction, as the girl left the room, thus imparting her feeling of disbelief to Africa.

CHAPTER 7

n spite of her successful day with all of its beautiful surprises, Africa was upset, when she climbed into bed. It was difficult for her to fall asleep. She lay there thinking.

A June wedding! Was it true? It had to be. The girl had no reason to lie. How could she? But why would Kevin date her, and treat her the way he had if he was engaged? How did he expect they would relate after his marriage? Trying to think of answers, she tossed and turned until she finally was worn out and fell asleep.

The next day should have been a beautiful one for Africa, but all the unanswered questions tormented her, so that she was too preoccupied to enjoy it's amazing events, as she would have liked to. It even started off with trouble. She rushed downstairs at seven on her way to the kitchen for coffee. When she approached the large, oak door, which opened into the kitchen, it was partially ajar, and she heard one voice, loud and sharp, from within.

"Now you remember what I just said, Lupe. I want no mistakes. No one is served in the dining room but the family, and guests, when I tell you. That maid Mother Hildenbrandt brought here is not included. She is not a member of this family or a guest. I don't want her served in my dining room! Is that clear, Lupe?"

"Si, Senora, si."

"Take her a tray upstairs before she gets down here, and tell her she is to have her meals served to her up there."

"Si, Senora, si. I understand."

Africa backed away, horrified. It had to be Kevin's mother, and her tone clearly indicated that she did not like her. Africa turned, and quickly ran through the corridor, and back upstairs to the sitting room.

I'll have to keep my distance from her, she thought, as she sat and began reading from her text book. Mrs. Hildenbrandt was asleep. Africa had arisen at five-thirty in order to give her patient a good, speedy, bath and prepare herself for school.

Mrs. Hildenbrandt's sharp eyes noticed the circles under Africa's eyes, and admonished her for worrying about the reported engagement and marriage between Kevin and Nanette.

"Shush, Child, Kevin's not studying about Nanette."

Lupe finally arrived with a delectable breakfast, but it all tasted like so much cotton and stuck in Africa's throat. One thing for sure, Kevin's mother would never accept his being engaged to her. She obviously felt Africa was not on her same level, and resented her even being in the house. How could there ever be anything meaningful between her and Kevin if his family felt this way about her, even if he wasn't engaged.

Jose drove Africa to school. It was a lovely, warm, sunshiny day. After class she rode with one of her classmates to the hospital where they were assigned for practical experience. Jose later picked her up and drove her home. She had decided to take this evening off, in order to pick up the necessary clothing, and other articles, she would need at the Hildenbrandt's. Lucy was thrilled at Africa's good fortune in having someone like Mrs. Hildenbrandt hire her. She and Brenda asked, what Africa determined was a million questions, about the Hildenbrandts. She finally asked them not to be so nosey. This was after they began questioning her about Kevin. She became quite agitated, told them he was just a friend, that she was tired, and went into the bedroom and retired, with her books, for the evening.

Lucy had told Billy about the car, so when he arrived home, later that night, he dashed into the bedroom, immediately, to see Africa, and in the process woke up Joey. Brenda had to get up to quiet the crying child, but none of this diverted Billy's attention from Africa propped up in bed, reading her lessons. She told him the story about Mrs. Hildenbrandt loaning her the car to get back and forth from school. Billy promised her, he would see that she obtained her drivers license before the next week was over.

"What's the matter, Sis? You ought to be jumping for joy," he said, after sensing a mood of depression about her.

"Nothing, Billy. I guess I'm just tired," she said, where upon, he left, after making her promise to cut out the light and go to sleep within five minutes. Both Joey and Brenda had gone back to sleep. Africa tried, but it took some time for her to drop off to sleep, and when she did, it was a restless sleep, filled with dreams which she couldn't recall the next morning.

The following afternoon, while Africa was giving Mrs. Hildenbrandt one of her very special back rubs, she heard laughter out by the pool. Looking across, she saw Mrs. Hildenbrandt Jr., Kevin's mother; Mark's wife, Jeannie, and Nanette. They were enjoying the pool and a lovely, warm afternoon. Lupe was serving them refreshments in tall glasses, and fruit salads. They seemed to be having a great time.

"Would you like to join them, dear?" asked Mrs. Hildenbrandt.

"Oh, no Mam."

"Not very friendly, are they?"

"Well, I really haven't seen anyone but Lupe and Jose since the other night, and today, I've only been here for an hour or so," said Africa.

"Well, they could have made some effort to be cordial. But, don't you worry, my Child. This is my house, and I'm giving you the run of it. You do anything that makes you happy, and go wherever you please."

"Thank you, Mrs. Hildenbrandt. You're so good to me. I'll never be able to thank you."

"No need. I need you, and I think you need me. That makes us tight," then referring to the back rub," That's enough of that now. Put on the news.

89

The world's coming apart. Glad I won't be around to see the finish."

"You can't go anywhere, Mrs. Hildenbrandt. Without you, I'd be, as my mother says, like a lost ball in high weeds. They both laughed cheerfully as Africa turned on the television and Mrs. Hildenbrandt remarked,

"She's about right, too."

Africa, dressed in night clothes, sat reading and taking notes, at the impressive, old mahogany desk. She knew it was a fine piece of furniture, as was everything else in the room. Just a short while earlier, she and Mrs. Hildenbrandt, had finished the delicious dinner Lupe had brought up to them. Now, Africa admired the fantastic mound of fresh fruit Lupe had prepared, especially for her, and placed on the desk. She munched on the grapes as she worked. Occasionally, she would catch her mind wandering back over the events of the day, and the week. One thing for certain, she had made up her mind not to do, and that was not to quit this job. She wouldn't leave Mrs. Hildenbrandt, as long as the dear woman wanted her to remain in her employ. Too much was dependent upon her salary, and Mrs. Hildenbrandt had made it possible for her to continue on in school. Kevin and the rest of the family would just have to accept her as an employee. Socializing with them was not her goal, and she would be very happy, just to stay in her quarters, and care for Mrs. Hildenbrandt. She would have to put Kevin out of her mind. That night, she managed to do so by studying until three o'clock in the morning. When she put down her books, and sleepily crawled into the bed, she made out earlier, in anticipation of this time, she immediately fell into a sound sleep.

The next morning, as Africa was preparing to leave for school, Mrs. Hildenbrandt asked that she hand her purse over to her. Africa had just administered her morning medication, and made the old lady comfortable for the day. Mrs. Hildenbrandt, searched her purse, then handed Africa a credit card. It bore the name of one of Beverly Hills' most exclusive women's stores.

"I know you and Kevin have a date Saturday night. You're a beautiful picture, dear, and I want you in a beautiful frame. Have Jose drop you off here to pick up something pretty to wear. Ask for Alice, she'll help you find something extra chic."

Africa was surprised. At first she refused, but after thinking about it, she really didn't have anything to wear and she had no money to buy anything. So, she accepted the card, and thanked Mrs. Hildenbrandt with a kiss and a happy smile.

It was a little past dinner time when Africa arrived home that evening. Jose let her out at the front door, and offered to bring her books and packages upstairs for her after he put the car in the garage. She accepted his offer for her books, but carried the packages with her new shoes and suit because she wanted to show them to Mrs. Hildenbrandt right away.

Using the key Mrs. Hildenbrandt had given her, she entered the vestibule and proceeded towards the staircase, when the gnawing in her stomach reminded her that she was indeed hungry. Just in case Jose takes his time, I'd better run back to the kitchen and let Lupe know I'm here, she thought. As she approached the dining room, she heard voices. The family was having dinner. Then, she detected a very familiar voice. Kevin was home. A bit of the conversation reached her ears; she did not intend to stop and listen, but her interest dictated otherwise. Kevin was speaking.

"Really, I don't know why Nanette has to hang around here all the time. Why do you encourage her, Mother?"

"Don't be ridiculous, Kevin. She and Terry have spent most of their lives in this house. We all like her. She's just like family."

"Well, after June, she'll be living here permanently, old man. So what's the problem?" asked Mark.

"Why? What's with June?" asked Kevin.

"Well, Son, that is your wedding date! Have you forgotten? She told Mama the other night."

"You know better than that! She's done it before. I'll have to speak to Nanette. I don't know anything about any engagement or marriage in June. She has to be losing her mind," said Kevin.

"Well, I'll say!" exclaimed Jeannie. "You're making a mistake, Kevin."

"Son, she's right for you. She's got everything... family, money, education and looks. What else do you want? And, she loves you too!" spoke his mother.

"Forget it, Mom," remarked Kevin. Africa detected agitation in his voice.

"Could that be because of your new interest, Son? Mama tells me you've got one," said Dr. Hildenbrandt.

"Oh!" exclaimed Jeannie. "Who is she?"

"Yes," remarked his mother in a sarcastic manner. "Is she rich? Who is her family?"

"Really, Gloria. Must you?" said Dr. Hildenbrandt.

"Kevin, is she anybody?" asked Jeannie.

"Is she anybody?" Kevin's voice was angry as he repeated Jeannie's question. "And all of us just one step out of slavery! Shit!"

"Jeannie, you talk too much," admonished Mark.

"Now, I've really lost my appetite," complained Kevin's father.

"And you a doctor?" remarked Gloria Hildenbrandt as she gave her husband a disgusted glance, then reprimanded Kevin with," Watch your mouth, Son. We are at the table. Kevin! Kevin!" she called.

Africa was out of sight, but not prepared for Kevin's quick exit. She did not have a chance to move, and once again they collided. He looked surprised to see her, and she was frightened to have him know that she had been listening. His dark eyes were brooding, and he quickly guided her across the hallway and into the study, a spacious and comfortably furnished room with floor to ceiling book cases stocked with hundreds of good books, luxurious tapestry, and rich walnut paneling.

Once inside, he closed the large double doors and stared at her.

Africa still clung to her packages. "Kevin I'm sorry. I didn't mean to listen. I was on my way to the kitchen, and..."

He interrupted, "I guess you heard everything."

"Yes, and it was interesting to learn about your engagement. I heard Nanette tell your grandmother all about it."

"Well, now you know," he said, smiling at her. "Everything happens for the best," he continued. "Now I don't have to explain."

"But, I never heard of anyone doing anything like that before. How could she?"

"Nanette has always had everything she's ever wanted. She doesn't understand, no, and she can't accept it either. Sometimes she feels that if she tells a lie, it will eventually come true."

"Kevin, how childish!"

"I agree," he said quietly.

"So, you're not getting married on June fifteenth?"

Kevin put both hands in his pockets as he began walking and talking.

"Of course not. I've known Nanette and her sister, Terry, all our lives. Their parents are publishers of the Los Angeles Tribune, the largest black newspaper in the west. They've always been terribly busy, and since we're next door neighbors, I grant you these houses have considerable space between, but nevertheless, Nanette and Terry spent a great deal of time here. My mom was always at home, and sometimes they were here from early morning until late at night. Mom enjoyed the girls. We belonged to the same clubs, same church, went to the same schools, name it, and our parents are close friends. They would like to hook the families up together, but it's never been unanimous with us kids. There you have it," sighed Kevin.

"I get the picture," said Africa moving closer to him. "And I see you catch on rather quickly too,"

Kevin looked puzzled.

"I thought I heard you cuss, so now we're even. You've picked up on my vulgarities."

"Oh, I'm sorry," said Kevin, somewhat embarrassed and laughing.

"Don't apologize," they both laughed. Then reaching out Kevin enfolded her into his arms, drawing her close to him. For a second they looked into each others eyes, in complete silence. Suddenly his head bent, and his lips were hungrily pressing hers. Her lips parted, the precious packages she held, and her purse fell to the floor, as her arms wound tightly around his neck. Their kiss was long and passionate.

A smothered cough and a male voice saying, "Kevin," broke through their moment of magic.

Both turned to see the older Dr. Hildenbrandt standing in the doorway.

"Better come on, Kevin, Mark's waiting in the car. We don't want to be late for the board meeting."

Although surprised, both Kevin and Africa collected themselves beautifully.

He kissed her tenderly on the cheek, then said, "I'll see you Saturday evening at six, Africa."

"O.K.," she said with a smile.

Quickly he retrieved her packages and purse from the floor, handed them to her, then went to join his father.

Looking at his son first, and then smiling at Africa, Dr. Hildenbrandt said, "Kevin, you always were a lucky rascal!"

Still smiling, Africa waved a good-bye to both of them, as they quickly departed the room.

Saturday couldn't come fast enough for Africa. She was only mildly disturbed to see Nanette all over the house when she came in on Friday. The three women had been to a luncheon, and fashion show together, and had made some purchases, which they were examining in the living room. Nanette was up and down the stairs, showing hers to Mrs. Hildenbrandt, who dismissed her when Africa arrived.

"That's enough now Nanette. Africa's here, and we've got a few things to do."

"Hi! Looks like you've had an interesting day," said Africa to Nanette, as she observed the dresses, the young woman was taking from the chaise lounge. Nanette only stared at Africa, and returned the warm greeting with an icy stare, and cold, "Hello." Then she rushed by her, as if avoiding something offensive. From the doorway, she cheerily called to Mrs. Hildenbrandt, "Mrs. Hildenbrandt asked me to stay for dinner, so I'll be here for awhile if you need me for anything."

"I hope not," mumbled the elder lady. Then she said to Africa, "You know I was in New Hope for five years, and nary a time did she darken my door. Now every time I look up there she is, pretending to want to do something for me. One of these days I'm going to fool her and ask her to empty my bedpan."

They could hear Nanette's high heels clicking across the vestibule's marble floor as she returned to the living room.

"Well, it's obvious what she thinks about me," sighed Africa.

"Don't let it bother you, Child. She gets on my nerves. Rattled brain, I call her. She's just jealous of you and all you've got going for you. She's frightened, with good cause."

"But, Mrs. Hildenbrandt, I don't have anything that she should be jealous of, really, I don't understand."

"Oh, dear," moaned the old lady, with exasperation.

"Just keep on thinking that way. It's part of your appeal. Don't try to understand anything about that one. It's not worth your while. Now, come on over here and help me," said Mrs. Hildenbrandt, as she reached for the overhead trapeze bar, and attempted to change her position, with a frown on her face.

"I'm tired out, and so uncomfortable. Let's get the show on the road!"

Africa immediately rushed to her side.

Saturday evening finally arrived, and Africa was ready at five. She stepped into Mrs. Hildenbrandt's room for inspection. The old lady was delighted.

"Just the look I wanted!" she exclaimed. "Your taste and mine run the same, Africa. I knew that was the right outfit for you the minute you showed it to me. Step around here and let me see the length." Africa moved to the spot she directed, and then heard Mrs. Hildenbrandt's zealous expression of, "Perfect!"

Africa had chosen a beautiful lavender, dressy suit with exquisite detail. It had a matching floral, chiffon blouse, with a low cut neckline. Alice had insisted on the high heeled, snake skin pumps in two shades of lavender. Africa was stunning and smart. The color blended perfectly with her smooth, rich skin, with its unusual radiance. Her dark, wavy hair was full of luster as it dropped casually about her shoulders. She smiled, as she was pleased with herself too.

"Do you think Kevin will like it?"

"I've never known that boy to ever be really sick, Child, and it's unlikely it will happen tonight. I'll bet he tells you he loves you tonight!"

"Oh, Mrs. Hildenbrandt, you're my fairy godmother. But that's too much to hope for."

"We'll see. Now look over there in my top drawer, and bring me that little black case from the right side."

Africa followed her instructions, and Mrs. Hildenbrandt opened the case, and brought forth the loveliest amethyst set of jewelry Africa could have ever imagined. There was a dainty, but beautifully cut, amethyst stone dangling from a gold chain, matching dangling earrings, and a precious, gold bracelet with several matching but smaller stones. When Mrs. Hildenbrandt directed her to put them on and wear them, Africa was breathless with excitement. The jewelry added just the right touch. Africa felt like a princess.

"If Kevin tells you he loves you tonight, they're yours," said Mrs. Hildenbrandt. There was a mischievous sparkle in her eyes.

Africa laughed in amazement, as she studied herself in the mirror.

"I can't lie, Mrs. Hildenbrandt. I wish they were mine, but I think you know when you're on safe ground."

Mrs. Hildenbrandt seemed not to hear her, as she said, "Africa, look in that same drawer again, there should be a brown envelope, where you found the jewelry case. Hand it to me please."

Africa again followed Mrs. Hildenbrandt's instructions. She watched the old lady open the envelope, and pull out a photograph. She handed it to Africa.

"Look at this," she commanded.

"I don't understand," said Africa. "It looks like me, but it's not me."

Africa studied the picture of a beautiful, young, woman dressed in clothing from during the nineteen twenties.

"Who is this girl, Mrs. Hildenbrandt?" she asked.

"Guess," Mrs. Hildenbrandt smiled and Africa knew.

"I used to be a pretty thing too, my child. When I first saw you, I was taken aback, because you reminded me of this picture. I have others, and you favor me in all of them. But the likeness is most striking in this particular one."

"It's incredible," said Africa. She returned the picture to Mrs. Hildenbrandt, who looked at it again, then settled comfortably back on her pillow.

"Kevin thinks so, too. Now doesn't that tell you something," she said with a satisfied smile. The two women were still talking when Kevin knocked and entered through the open sitting room door.

"Everybody decent?" he called. He kissed his grandmother in greeting, then stood by Africa, slipping his arm about her waist. He kissed her on the cheek, then said, "Uhumm umumm, you smell as good as you look, and that's beautiful."

Africa gave a demure smile as she said, "Thank you, Kevin."

They were on their way down the stairs, when Kevin's mother, Gloria, standing at the bottom of the stairway confronted them. She was handsomely gowned, and her expression clearly indicated her displeasure.

"Well, what is this?" she asked.

"Hi, Mother. I missed you when I came in. Africa and I have a date tonight. Neither of us will be here for dinner. I've told Lupe already," said Kevin.

"That's not the point, Kevin. I see you so seldom these days, although you're right here in town. The whole family misses your company. You have so few evenings free, and yet you choose to go out, rather than spend it with your family. I invited Nanette and Terry to dinner too." She seemed to ignore Africa completely as they stood in the vestibule.

"Sorry, Mother, but I didn't invite them, so I feel no obligation. Africa and I have plans."

"Hello, Mrs. Hildenbrandt," spoke Africa. This was the first time she had seen the woman all day.

"Well, hello. I thought you were attending to Mother in the evenings. I'm concerned that you have your obligations confused," she said coldly to Africa.

"This is my evening off," answered Africa.

"Well, I'm surprised you didn't go home. I'm certain your family must miss you, too."

"Look, Mother, I'm sure they do, but I think they'll manage to forgive me for wanting to be with their lovely Africa this evening." He smiled at Africa, then taking her by the arm, he said,

"See you later, Mother. Have a good evening," and he led Africa to the front door. As they departed, she looked back to see an angry Mrs. Hildenbrandt turn in the upstairs' hallway towards the senior Mrs. Hildenbrandt's rooms.

"You'll have to forgive Mother, Africa." said Kevin as they drove away from the house. "Sometimes I don't think she can accept me and Mark being grown up."

"It's O.K., Kevin. I understand," said Africa, and to herself, she thought, and understand, I do, your mother doesn't think I'm good enough for you. She doesn't like me one bit. Wonder how she would feel about me if I were to suddenly inherit a large sum of money and become rich like Nanette?

"I'd like to take you to one of my favorite eating places," Kevin told Africa. "I'm anxious, and starving," she said.

The place Kevin had in mind was a beautiful oriental restaurant, nestled high in the Hollywood Hills. Their dinner was served by gracious waiters, and waitresses dressed in the clothing of their homeland. The atmosphere, decor, and music were so original, that Africa felt as if she had taken a quick trip and been transported to Japan. It was all so enchanting. The garden table, which they occupied, afforded them an eagle's eye view of Hollywood, and greater Los Angeles.

During the many courses of the most delicious oriental food that Africa had ever tasted, Kevin gave her insight into the type of life which he had lived. He had mostly attended private schools, and had graduated from Howard University, from which his parents had also graduated. There, he had met friends from all over the United States, and he had visited them in most of the eastern states, North and South, and even Texas. Africa was fascinated to learn of his travels abroad, starting at an early age. As an exchange student, he had lived one year in Paris, and spoke fluent French. He also spoke German and Spanish. Japan had been one of his parent's favorite places to vacation, and he also shared their love for the Orient. He had been there half a dozen times, and enjoyed coming to this particular restaurant, since it reminded him so much of that country.

Africa found Kevin to be extremely devoted to medicine. He wanted to work among the poor and disadvantaged. He mentioned his uncle in Georgia, who was a surgeon and the owner of a community hospital. He had worked with him during the summers, while in medical school. It was his dream to return to Georgia to practice, after he finished his residency program, and became a surgeon. This was his last year, and this summer he would complete his training. Africa listened to him with the greatest fascination, because she shared his feelings of working with the underprivileged.

"There's so much to be done for our people, Africa. So many of them feel that if they go to a doctor, he might find something fatally wrong, or that a hospital is a place where you go to die. So they never seek medical attention until things are really bad. Surgery is then very complicated, and a definite challenge. When you can heal, then you've converted, not just one, but a whole family, or even a clan, to the value of health care. By saving one life you can, more or less, insure life to others."

"Kevin, it sounds wonderful. You can really feel you've done something. You can see it, and you know your sacrifice will help others who need you. It sounds like a great life." Africa was radiant with excitement as she finished.

"It doesn't mean as much money, as working in a big city, Africa. But satisfaction would be worth money to me."

"Kevin, you're a wonderful person," she told him.

As they were leaving, Africa was surprised to hear Kevin speak in Japanese, to a quite elderly Japanese man, whom he introduced to her as the owner of the establishment. He later explained that the man was a good friend of the Hildenbrandt family, and had carried out a business relationship with the elder, deceased Mr. Hildenbrandt. It was through him that the family's first visits to Japan had been arranged, and they had been guests in the home of his relatives frequently, while visiting his homeland.

After their delightful dinner experience, Kevin took Africa to the Shubert Theater to see the musical, "Dream Girls". The cast was superb, the music, singing , and dancing terrific. Since they both could identify with the plot and jokes as portrayed by the black actors, their enjoyment was intense. They intermittently laughed, then they swayed in response to the music, or they sat on the edge of their seats enjoying the on stage excitement. Afterwards, they had a good time laughing and kidding about the plays merits, as they evaluated it over coffee, and dessert in a near by ice cream parlor.

Africa felt a warm glow of comfort and happiness, as Kevin turned his key in the lock at the gate. It quickly opened, and he drove slowly up the driveway to the house. He opened the door for her, and she stepped out of the car into the driveway. The night was beautiful with a full, mellow moon which shone through the swaying palm trees, against the backdrop of a star studded sky. Crickets chirped a melodious tune, and the fragrance of roses and gardenias perfumed the air.

"Kevin," Africa uttered in awe, "It's such a lovely night. Look at that moon! It's so bright and there are a million stars. Tomorrow will be another beautiful day. I plan to go to church."

"I'd love to go with you, but I have rounds every morning at seven."

He gave her his heartwarming smile and continued, "Both you and the night are beautiful, Africa."

Their goodnight kiss, just before Kevin opened the front door, opened Pandora's Box. The evening had been everything they could have wanted it to be, but Kevin revealed his longing, when he whispered to her, "After that kiss, Honey, I realize I've wasted an entire evening."

Africa's answer was to offer her lips to him again, and both moaned slightly at the ecstasy which engulfed them. Kevin sighed as he released her, and opened the door. The great crystal chandelier, which graced the magnificent stairway was turned down low. The light cast by its hundreds of tiny crystals was ethereal, as it dimly lighted a richly carpeted path to the second floor.

Kevin closed the door quietly behind them, then he swept Africa with his fascinating eyes, and finally captured her eyes with his.

"Look, Baby," he spoke softly. His rich, masculine voice excited her. "There's something I've wanted to say all evening, but I just didn't seem to find the right time."

"What is it, Kevin?" she asked, moving closer to him. There was a concerned, inquisitiveness in her eyes as she came nearer to him. Once again, he held her in his arms. He buried his face in her hair, and she felt a deeper rapture race through her as his lips moved close to her ear.

"Africa, I love you," he whispered. Honey, "I'm head over heels in love with you. I want you so very much, and I need you. There's no one else I want but you. I'll always be miserable until you're mine."

Again their lips met, tenderly and sweetly. His hands caressed her body, and she felt a shiver of excitement race down her spine. This time it was

Africa who interrupted their growing desire. She pulled away from him, feeling a poignant ache as she did so. Their eyes met in the semi-darkness, and she could feel her heart pounding.

"I love you too, Kevin. I, I," she stammered in frustration then finally said, "Good night, Kevin," and raced up the stairs and into her room, shutting the door softly behind her. She could hear Mrs. Hildenbrandt snoring lightly in the next room. Quickly she undressed and slipped into a shimmering, soft, white satin gown, another gift from Mrs. Hildenbrandt . Then she made out her bed and lay the matching peignoir across the foot. Once under the covers, Africa suddenly remembered that she had not removed her jewelry. Just as suddenly she sat up in bed and giggled softly with joy.

"They're mine! Mine! Mine!," she repeated to herself as she felt the amethyst necklace, earrings, and bracelet Mrs. Hildenbrandt had insisted that she wear earlier that evening.

"He said it! He said it! He loves me. Thank you, my dear Kevin. They're mine, and you love me!"

Removing her gifts carefully, she placed them under her pillow. Falling back on the same soft pillow, she closed her eyes while her mind raced over the beauty of the evening and its glorious ending, she had just spent with Kevin. But why did she run away from him? I love him, she thought, but I'm afraid. Whatever would have happened next, I was not ready for it. I was afraid, but why?, she asked herself. It's bound to happen with Kevin. I love him and he loves me. He said it. I feel he has to be telling the truth. While pondering her action and feelings, Africa dropped off to sleep.

Suddenly, she was awakened by a vigorous shaking of her bed. In the light from the adjoining bathroom she could see that the whole room was in motion. There was a creaking sound of lumber, and the rattling of window panes, which seemed to come from all over the big house. She could hear a rumbling sound and the crash of falling articles. A picture fell from the wall. She knew it was an earthquake. The light in Mrs. Hildenbrandt's bathroom and hers went out, and both rooms were left in darkness. The shaking continued, and she feared that if it kept on the whole house would cave in.

"Please, dear Lord, let it stop," she prayed, as she quickly jumped out of bed and rushed to the door. But before she could turn the knob, it had stopped, and all was quiet, quieter than before, an eerie kind of quietness. She hugged herself in fear.

"Thank you, Jesus, thank you for stopping it," she muttered. Her heart was racing from the fear she experienced. There was a quick jolt.

"Please, Lord, don't let it start again," she prayed.

Turning about, she rushed towards Mrs. Hildenbrandt's bedroom. It was dark and she could not see into the room, but she could hear Mrs. Hildenbrandt still snoring. Evidently her patient had slept through the whole episode and had not heard or felt a thing. She always did sleep well at night, thought Africa. She attributed it to the rather large dose of Choral Hydrate prescribed for her at bedtime. Too bad I didn't sleep through it, she thought, closing the door between the two rooms. If Mrs. Hildenbrandt needed her, she had a brass bell within her reach that she could shake, and also the velvet cord which resounded throughout the entire house.

Suddenly, it occurred to her that she must call home. She reached for the phone, but realized she couldn't see to dial. Quickly, she opened the shutters on the windows next to her bed and moonlight poured in and brightened the room, but not enough that she could read to dial. Suddenly, the door from the hallway opened, and a flash light shone into the room.

"Africa! Africa, are you all right?"

It was Kevin.

"Oh, yes, Kevin. I'm all right, just scared. Earthquakes are one of the few things that really scare me."

He drew her to him, in an effort to comfort her.

"How's Grandma?" he asked.

"Kevin, can you believe it? She's still asleep. She slept through it all!"

Kevin chuckled in relief. Another flash light approached them. It was Dr. Hildenbrandt.

"Everybody O.K.?" he asked. "How's Mama?" he continued before either could answer.

"Africa's pretty well frightened, but I think that's all. Grandma didn't budge, Dad, and she's still asleep," answered Kevin. After Kevin's report the senior Dr. Hildenbrandt called to his wife, Gloria, and others, who were standing somewhere in the hallway.

"Man, that was a good one! Haven't felt one like that in years! Everybody O.K.?"

Africa heard Jose answer from downstairs. "Si, everybody's O.K."

"Let's all go back to bed. Mama didn't even wake up. The electricity will hopefully be restored by morning," called Dr. Hildenbrandt again. There

113

was the sound of laughter when Jeannie reported that Mark never got out of bed.

"That guy, he never lets anything bother him. Now that's what I call "laid back", remarked Kevin, as he laughed heartily about his brother.

With the help of Kevin's flashlight, Africa dialed home.

"We're all O.K., Mom. I'm so glad you are too. Yes, that was a pretty rough one. No, I can't remember a worse one either. I'm still shaking. Yes, of course, I'll be there for church. Jose will drive me over, but Billy will have to run him back so I can keep the car. Tell him he'll have to bring me back about seven, and catch the bus back home. I know you're not going, but I wish you were. All right, all right, Mom. I understand. I know you would go if you could. Maybe one day you'll get better. Tell Brenda to have Joey dressed and herself ready by ten-thirty. We don't want to be late. I'll be there by nine. It's O.K., Mom. I'll replace your broken dishes and whatever else. Don't worry, now. It's all over. Love you. See you in the morning. Bye."

Kevin stood above Africa, as she sat on the edge of her bed and talked to her mother. When she finished, he placed the phone on the receiver. Gently pulling her to her feet, he enfolded her into his arms.

"Hey, Honey. you are shaking," he spoke softly.

He held her close to him as if she were a child, gently stroking her temples, and brushing back her hair. She could feel the fear slowly drain from her body and become replaced by a growing desire. Kevin released her for a moment in which he closed the hallway door and cut off his flashlight which lay on the bed. In the moonlight she could see his broad, muscular chest. He wore only pajama bottoms, and his feet were bare as they touched hers. Again she was in his arms. This time their lips met with deep passionate kisses. The softness and sweetness of his mouth was unbelievable to her, and she could only clamor for more of him. Oh, Kevin, you must never let me go, she was thinking over and over in her mind.

When he replied, "I won't, my Love, I won't," she realized she must have spoken aloud.

Africa felt him lift the straps of her gown from her shoulders, and felt the softness of satin about her feet, as it slipped to the floor. Her body was illuminated in the moonlight, which shone through the window. She was a silhouette of beauty. Kevin's eyes devoured her firm breasts, narrow waist line, the voluptuous swelling of her hips, and the sensuous curves of well proportioned thighs and lovely legs.

He spoke softly as he told her, "My God, Africa, you are a beautiful work of art. I knew you were lovely, but my imagination didn't stretch this far, and believe me, I see a hell of a lot."

She smiled up at him and whispered, "O.K., Kevin, let's get the show on the road!"

Kevin seemed quietly surprised for a moment, then smothered a chuckle.

"I always thought there was a bit of witch in you. It's obvious with whom you're been hanging out," he whispered, drawing her close to him again. They both laughed, but their humor ceased as he kissed her mouth, and then her eyes, her ears, neck and then passionately and tenderly, he kissed her breasts. Africa felt her breath come in gasps. Kevin's moans of pleasure and desire thrilled her even more. She was aware when his pajama bottoms joined her gown, and he held her incredibly close.

"Oh, Honey," he whispered between kisses. You feel so good close to me like this. We're meant for each other."

Africa felt her body mold to his in a very sensual perfection. Their hearts seemed to beat as one. Gently he lowered her to the bed. Their passion grew as Kevin's kisses and tender caresses ignited a fire which began to rage within her. His hands gently claimed her satiny skin. Suddenly, Africa froze.

"Kevin, I can't," she whispered.

In the moonlight, she clearly saw the puzzled expression on his handsome face. He looked into her eyes.

"What is it, my Love?" he whispered.

"I'm afraid, Kevin. I've never, well.. I, I...It's my first time."

For a second Kevin was quiet. Then he held her closer as he whispered, "Africa, you're full of surprises. You always seemed so hip."

He kissed her tenderly.

"I would never hurt you, Honey, you should know that. I'm glad you told me. I love you so much. Just relax, and trust me."

His kisses began again, tender, gentle, and sweet. Her body melted, and then was consumed with the flames of desire, which cried out from the depths of her being for fulfillment. Once, Africa thought she experienced a twinge of pain. She was not sure and didn't care, because she only existed for the fierce passion, incredible ecstasy and glorious satisfaction of their love.

It was early morning when Africa awakened. The events of the night before came into focus. She determined that the lights were on again, as hers shone in the room. Turning, she reached out for Kevin, but he was not there. She looked at the clock on the bedside table. It read five-thirty. Languorously, she turned over again to recapture the incredible rapture of the past few hours.

CHAPTER 8

frica gave Mrs. Hildenbrandt her morning bath, and made her comfortable. It was during the process, that the old lady asked, "Well, Child, do I get back my jewelry, or do you keep it?'

Africa smiled, then clasped her patient's plump, age speckled hand into both of hers as she replied, "Thank you, Mrs. Hildenbrandt. They're mine. He said it! He said he loves me, and I'm so happy! They're mine!" They hugged each other, and the older woman said, "You're going to be my grand-daughter, yet. You've got great spirit in you, Child, and this family needs an infusion. Looks like we've got love on the road!"

After her shower, Africa dressed in a pretty beige suit, and hat she brought from home. The outfit was old, but still in style. The high neck of lace ruffles on the blouse along with her upswept hairstyle, made her look as if she were from another generation. Mrs. Hildenbrandt admired the look.

"You're the picture of me, when I was your age, Child," she mused.

It was eight o'clock when Africa rushed down the stairs on her way to meet Jose, who was waiting with the car in the driveway. Billy had kept his promise to help her, and she would probably get her driver's license the coming week. Mrs. Hildenbrandt had instructed Jose to chauffeur her as needed, and he had been extremely patient and kind. She had become very fond of him and Lupe. They did everything possible to insure her comfort. She was on her way out the front door, when Mark stopped her.

"Good morning, Africa. You look great. Going to church?"

"Thank you, Mark," she spoke with a beautiful smile. "You're right, I'm on my way to church with my family. That's my brother, my sister and my little nephew. We usually go every Sunday."

"Now, that's wonderful. Sounds like you have a fine family."

"I think so. There's my mom, too, but she's been ill and can't go with us now. We have hopes for the future."

"Sorry to hear that, but I'm sure everything will work out for all of you soon. Going to church is a family habit here, too. Look, give this card to your sister's boyfriend, Moses. Kevin told me about him, and I'd like to see if I can put him to work with the company. Have him call me about nine-thirty tomorrow," he directed.

Africa was so surprised and pleased. She was at a loss for words. Her eyes suddenly glistened, and she was afraid she might cry with happiness. Kevin was so wonderful, she thought.

"Thank you, Mr. Hildenbrandt. Oh, thank you so very much! I'll see that he gets this right away."

After church, when Billy drove the car into the driveway, they found Moses waiting for them, sitting on the front steps. Lucy still would not permit him in the house. He greeted them, kissing Brenda and little Joey. Africa immediately gave him the card and Mark's directions. Brenda was so excited she started jumping up and down.

"Wait up a minute, Woman, I ain't got nothing, yet," Moses told her with a grin, "But I'm gonna sure be there early!"

Later that evening when Africa returned to her room, she found a beautiful vase of red roses on her desk. She was so thrilled that her fingers shook when she picked the small white envelope from amidst the green leaves and baby breath. She opened the envelope and pulled out the small white card, which read:

"To my Africa, the sweetest, most beautiful girl in the world.

Love, Kevin"

Her eyes became misty. She was surprised at herself for loving any man as much as she did Kevin. He was indeed her Knight in Shining Armor. Just the thought of him and the love they shared the night before, sent her pulses racing and made the world brighter, more beautiful and exciting than she ever imagined it could be.

The next evening, Kevin called.

"Hi, Sweetheart! I'm missing you so much it hurts." She could sense the emotion in his voice and told him she felt the same way. Heexplained that he was very busy but thought of her all the time. They talked and laughed about their day to day routine. Africa was excited about taking her driver's test the next afternoon, and Kevin was excited about his work in general. They decided on a date for Thursday, Kevin's afternoon off. They would dress in shorts and go bike riding along the beach. Kevin said he needed the exercise and Africa agreed it wouldn't do her any harm. Their conversation ended with Kevin telling her how slow the time would go for him until he could be with her again. Their expressions of love to each other, left her pulses racing.

Billy lived up to his word. Between help from him and Jose, Africa passed her driver's test and obtained her license the next afternoon. Billy had taken her to the Department of Motor Vehicles, therefore she had to drop him off at home before returning to the Hildenbrandts. Lucy insisted she sit in the kitchen with her and celebrate by eating a piece of lemon meringue pie she had just made from the lemons she picked from their back yard tree. The pie was still warm and delicious. Lucy could make the flakiest, most tasty pie crust anyone ever touched with a fork.

"How's it going out there at the Hildenbrandt's?" she asked Africa.

"Fine, Mom. I don't see much of the family. They're usually always asleep when I get up in the morning, and out when I get there in the afternoon. Then in the evenings, I'm busy with Mrs. Hildenbrandt or studying."

"What about Kevin?" asked Lucy.

"He's seldom home, Mom. He has to stay at the hospital, because he's on call night and day most of the time. I don't think he gets much sleep at all."

123

"Well, you just make sure that when he does, he doesn't get it with you. I've never been too happy about a young girl living in around a lot of men, and particularly when I know she's stuck on one of them."

"Oh, Momma!"

"Oh, Momma nothing! I know what can happen. They can come creeping and crawling around at night, and any girl, as pretty as you, has to be on her guard. Rich or poor, they all crawl just the same."

"Kevin told me he loves me, Mom. We're in love."

"Don't you be no fool, Africa! If he loves you, let him marry you or make plans to do so soon. At least get a ring on your finger. Now I'm telling you to be careful. Why should a man buy the cow when he can get the milk free. So you just watch out. I don't want no more Brenda mess around this house. If it wasn't that I trusted Mrs. Hildenbrandt to look out for you, I'd make you come on back home."

"And then I wouldn't be able to continue on in school. Our bills wouldn't get paid either. Come on, Mom, be realistic."

"There's always Chuck Wilson. I'm still sorry you wouldn't take my advice there. You know he called here the other day."

"For what?" asked Africa in a flat tone.

"Well, he wanted to know how you were doing over there at the Hildenbrandts'."

"For Pete's sake! What did you tell the rascal?"

"Now that's no way to talk about him, Africa. I said, O.K., I'd 'spect, since you were still there. We had a long talk about his family and all. He sure is a nice young man."

"Can't stand him," muttered Africa.

"Girl, you just won't listen, will you! Got a head that's hard as a rock." Lucy's voice conveyed a hint of anger.

"Mom, that was the best pie ever." said Africa, abruptly changing the subject and jumping up from the table. "I've got to run now. Mrs. Hildenbrandt is waiting for me. I'll see you soon."

She kissed Lucy good-bye, and ran out to the car just in time to meet Brenda pushing Joey in his stroller, up the sidewalk. They were returning from their daily walk. Brenda was happy about Africa being able to drive, and stood by as Billy gave her a few last minute instructions before she pulled off.

Lucy called from the front porch, "Don't forget what I said, Africa Jones!"

Africa was irritated with her mother as she drove away. Why would she even bother to talk with Chuck? She thought Lucy definitely had an uncanny talent for figuring things out, but also, she was hasty in drawing the wrong conclusions. Now she had succeeded in making Africa feel a bit insecure about Kevin, thus upsetting her. Turning the radio up high, she drove back to the Hildenbrandts' trying to erase any distrust of Kevin from her mind. She indulged herself in their beautiful moments of the past, while anticipating more to come. Nevertheless, by the time she opened the gate with the new key Mrs. Hildenbrandt had presented to her for that purpose, and driven the car into the driveway, she had made a definite decision.

It bothered her that she and Kevin had been intimate, and although he said he loved her, he had not mentioned marriage or even an engagement. These facts made her uneasy. Because of this feeling, and some guilt too, she decided that until he did make some positive signs of commitment to her, there would be no more sex between them. Lucy's words rang in her ears. She knew she could not be at peace with herself if she succumbed again without

126

commitment. "Please, Lord, help me resist," she prayed silently to herself.

Nanette was leaving the house with Jeannie, when she arrived. Her car was parked in the driveway. Jeannie spoke cordially to Africa, but Africa's friendly,

"Hello! How are you?" to Nanette, did not receive a response. She only gave a cold stare, and then spoke loudly to Jeannie.

"You know, Jeannie, our servants always use the back door."

Africa was upset when she arrived at Mrs. Hildenbrandt's bedside. The older woman sensed her mood and lay the book she had been reading on her chest.

All right, Africa, tell me what's wrong. I'll bet it has something to do with that Nanette. She just left here worrying the hell out'ta me, talking a lot about absolutely nothing. Said she and Jeannie were on their way to a Dame's meeting. I've belonged to that club for fifty years, and you don't know how happy I am to have stopped going to meetings before that crew started."

Africa finally told Mrs. Hildenbrandt how Nanette acted, and what she had said. Mrs. Hildenbrandt smiled, as she said, "Don't let it bother you, Child. I told you she was silly. Some people have to be taught respect."

"Well, I don't intend to teach her anything."

"You don't know that. You never know what you might do."

Africa thought that Mrs. Hildenbrandt sometimes talked in riddles. She proceeded to make her patient comfortable for the night.

Nearly every afternoon, when Africa arrived from school, Nanette was at the house, playing tennis, swimming or having lunch with Jeannie and Gloria Hildenbrandt. Sometimes her sister, Terry, would be there, also. Their voices could be heard amid laughter through Mrs. Hildenbrandt's open bedroom window. It seemed to Africa that Thursday would never arrive. Then finally it had come, and Africa was preparing for her date with Kevin. She rushed to replace the nail file she had borrowed from Mrs. Hildenbrandt's bedside table.

"Come here, Child," commanded the old lady, and she grabbed Africa by the waist. "You can't go out of here with tags on you like that. People will think you're from the country."

Africa laughed as Mrs. Hildenbrandt released a tag attached to the rear waist of the yellow shorts she had purchased on her way from school. Today was her half day in class, and because of a change in schedule, she didn't have to do lab work at the hospital on Thursdays

"I don't know what you'd do without me," chided Mrs. Hildenbrandt.

Africa was serious as she replied, "Me either."

"Come on, now, Child. Get the show on the road. Kevin will be here any minute."

Africa straightened her shorts after Mrs. Hildenbrandt had finished removing the tag and its threads.

"I do wish Nanette wasn't here today. Do you think it will be a problem?" she asked the old lady, unable to conceal the anxiety in her voice.

"Don't worry, Honey. The only problem Nanette is going to cause will be for herself." Then quickly changing the subject, she smiled at Africa.

"Girl, you look like a million dollars! That yellow really becomes you. With legs like yours, I wouldn't be caught in a dress."

Africa smiled as she glanced in the dresser mirror. "You're just prejudiced, Mrs. Hildenbrandt," responded Africa, but she was pleased with what she saw. She wore a white tank top, trimmed in yellow. A predominately yellow, multi-colored scarf framed her soft, beautiful features and partially covered her dark hair, which fell in deep waves to her shoulders. Barely visible socks, sported yellow balls, which bobbed out the heels of her tennis shoes.

There was a knock at the sitting room door. They both jumped excitedly, knowing it was Kevin. Africa rushed to open the door.

"Hi!" he said, then gave a low whistle, as he stood sweeping his eyes over Africa.

She stared back at him. "Hi, Kevin."

He reached out, and brought her into his arms. "Baby, you're looking goooood!"

They kissed passionately. "Kevin, I've missed you so," whispered Africa. He assured her that he had missed her more. Then hand in hand they entered Mrs. Hildenbrandt's bedroom.

"I wondered if you were going to make it in here," she said, pretending to scold them. Africa only smiled, while Kevin greeted his grandmother with a joyous, "Hi, Grandma!" as he strode to her bedside, and gave her a kiss on the cheek and a big hug which she lovingly returned.

"Kevin, you do look sharp. I can see why Africa can't resist you."

Again Africa only smiled her approval. Kevin was so handsome in his khaki shorts and white tee shirt, that she was temporarily overwhelmed with his virile good looks. He wore an intricately marked sweat band about his forehead, which afforded him a Bohemian and mystic air. Africa felt he was everything she had dreamed about or hoped for.

"You plan to ride the bike trail down by the beach, Kevin?" asked Mrs. Hildenbrandt.

"Where else, Grandma" That's where you and Grandpa taught Mark and me to ride. Boy, did we have fun!"

"And did we," she agreed.

Africa's eyes were bright as she listened and laughed with them as they filled her in on their good times at the beach. Kevin's mother and father were usually too busy to go with them. Their father had a demanding practice to care for and their mother was very involved with her clubs or some other volunteer projects claimed most of her time. So Kevin and Mark spent much time with their grandparents, particularly Grandma Hildenbrandt. Finally Mrs. Hildenbrandt sent them off, while Africa was still giggling about some of their hilarious escapades. As they passed through the sitting room, Nanette rushed in from the hallway.

"Kevin!" she exclaimed.

She wore a wet bathing suit and her hair was curly with damp ringlets. Completely ignoring Africa, she threw her arms tightly about Kevin's neck, and standing on her tiptoes, she pulled his head downward and planted a kiss on his lips. Africa felt the blood rush to her face. She was both angry and jealous.

Unwinding Nanette's arms from about him, Kevin laughed and said, "Hi, Nan. Why so rambunctious?"

"I'm just glad to see you, Kevin. It's been a whole week, you know." For the first time she seemed to take notice of Africa, who moved from behind Kevin close to his side.

"Hello, Nanette," spoke Africa.

"Where are you going?" Nanette asked Kevin, her pretty face in a frown and completely ignoring Africa.

"We're on our way to the beach to do a little bike riding." answered Kevin.

"With her?" Nanette gave Africa a disdainful glance.

"Grandma and I thought Africa might like a little exercise too."

"Well , wait for me. I'd like to join you," said Nanette.

"You look like you're all ready too! Sorry, Nan, not this time."

"Nanette! Nanette!" It was Mrs. Hildenbrandt calling from the bedroom.

"Better check, Grandma," directed Kevin, as he took Africa's hand and hastened from the room.

"She's the nurse, not me!" They could hear Nanette repeating as they rushed through the hallway and down the stairs. Mrs. Hildenbrandt was persistently calling Nanette as they went out the front door. Her calling chimes sounded throughout the house.

Africa was surprised to find two neat five speed bicycles attached to Kevin's Mercedes. They laughed and teased all the way to the beach. When Kevin first leaned over to kiss her at the red light, Africa withdrew. Kevin looked puzzled, as she took a square packet from her purse. Opening it, she quickly wiped his mouth with a damp towelette. Kevin laughed all the way to the next stop light, where Africa allowed him to kiss her and then she snuggled closer to him.

Africa was delightfully surprised when Kevin told her the bicycle she was to ride was his gift to her. She could tell it was terribly expensive and the finest she had ever seen. Kevin's bicycle was the male counterpart. The bicycles were a joy to ride. They cycled from the Marina to Venice, a nearby beach town. They followed a well worn trail. The air was fresh and clean, and Africa's hair blew in the breeze which drifted in from the ocean. The warm sun caressed them and effortlessly darkened every exposed part of their well formed bodies. It was a heavenly day. The ocean sparkled and glimmered in the sunlight, which it seemed to meet on the horizon. They chained their bikes to a fence, and after removing their socks and shoes, walked across the warm sand to let the waves die out in a foamy splash over their bare feet. It was glorious, and their laughter reflected the happiness they felt in sharing the beauty of it all.

They ate lunch at a small sidewalk cafe. The area was like a beehive with other cyclist, roller skaters, nearly nude bathers, children, and beach comers. Music, laughter and an air of freedom permeated the atmosphere, and they enjoyed eating and watching the sights afforded in the little beach town.

Africa told Kevin her good news. Brenda had called her early that morning, so excited she could hardly talk straight, to let her know that Moses had been hired to work at the bank. He was being trained as a teller, and the whole family was delighted.

"He's really got a good mind, Kevin. Brenda says he's fantastic with figures."

"I'm sure Mark must have discovered that. Great! Now let's see what he'll do about Brenda and Joey," he told her.

"Here's some more good news," she told him as they were leaving the cafe. She handed him a white envelope, which he opened to find an invitation to her graduation.

"I hope you can come," she said.

"I will," he answered giving her an affectionate kiss.

They ate pizza, drank sodas, licked ice cream cones, and devoured big bags of popcorn which they carried in the baskets on their bikes, as they laughed and cycled for hours like two excited children. Africa's stamina and endurance for fun, on their long excursion, seemed to astonish Kevin.

With their bikes neatly stored in the rack over the trunk, Kevin drove his SL450 carefully on the freeway, homeward bound. The small car was easy to handle, and Kevin quickly reached the speed limit, as he prepared to move into the fast lane. There was a deafening bang, like a shotgun blast. The car in front of them swerved out of control and Kevin instinctively pressed his brakes. He stopped the car a few feet short of the hood belonging to the crippled Ford, which had turned horizontally between two lanes. There was a loud crash and

135

before their eyes the Ford rocked from the impact of a small car, which obviously had not been able to stop quickly enough to avoid the accident. The Ford rolled over, and ended upside down, its wheels, including the flat, in an eerie spin. Kevin jumped from the car, his door just missing another car, which had come to a halt beside his. They later discovered that the fellow driving, had been directly behind them, and being unable to stop when Kevin had quickly applied his brakes, he had managed to pull over into the next lane and avoid a collision with them. Kevin and the fellow rushed to the upturned car. Africa followed. There were two passengers inside, held in place, upside down, by their seat belts. One was a very pregnant young woman, and the other a young man struggling to free himself.

"Help me!" he cried. "My wife's in labor. We were on our way to the hospital."

While the men attempted to free the woman, Africa stepped over, and looked into the small car, which had struck the couple. The occupant, a man, was slumped over the steering wheel. She lifted his head and blood was oozing from a deep gash at this temple. He appeared dead. Africa felt for a pulse. There was none. Another man had arrived and a woman behind her was screaming.Africa looked for

Kevin and saw him and two men lifting the woman out the window of the overturned car. Maybe this man isn't really dead yet, she thought. I've got to give him artificial respiration, and get his heart going before there's brain damage.

"Please help! We've got to get him out of there and on the ground, but quick!" she cried to the man next to her. With great haste, she jumped into the car, scrambled behind the injured man and then over into the passenger seat. He was limp, but she was determined it would not be harmful to move him if it were done carefully. With the help of others that arrived, she was able to get the man on the ground. Quickly she placed her mouth over his and began to blow. She felt, and there was no carotid pulse. It took her only a moment to move into position and start the vital chest compressions which would circulate blood throughout his still body. She noticed that the woman, who had been screaming, was now wiping the blood from the man's face and trying to stop the bleeding from the wound on his forehead.

Africa was busy counting as she gave the compressions. After she had administered fifteen, she would again breath into the man's mouth. He seemed to be about her age, and she felt desperately that he must live. It was time for her to breathe again for the man, when she saw Kevin appear. He dropped to his knees, and did it for her. Afterwards, there was still no pulse.

"Let me take over for you, Africa. I know you're tired. See to the pregnant woman over there. She's crowning and the baby will pop any minute."

"O.K.," she muttered, scrambling to her feet.

"Watch for the cord. Use the knife only if it's wrapped tight around the neck, and don't forget to make two knots with your shoelaces around the cord and cut in between," he cautioned her as he proceeded with the compressions to the young man's chest. Africa was relieved to see that a motorcycle policeman had arrived and he was using his radio to call for the paramedics. She looked at the woman, her legs were bent and parted. She grunted loudly and Africa could see the crown of the baby's head. Kevin had apparently quickly prepared the spot for birth. A blanket was beneath the woman, and a towel and tablecloth, which must have been in one of the cars, was beside her. A pocket knife lay near one foot. Again the woman grunted and then she screamed. Africa supported the baby's head as it burst from the vagina. She felt for the umbilical cord. It was not around the neck.

"Thank God," she whispered. Then on her knees, she helped the mother bring her infant into the world.

"He's breathing, Africa. We got him started again." It was Kevin. She looked up into his face and handed him the new baby boy. Kevin grasped the baby and held it, much like a football player cradles a football, along the length of his lower arm, with its head tilted down. He swept his finger inside the baby's mouth. There was little response, only several small whimpers. With his free hand, he managed to gently, but firmly, strike the bottom of both the baby's feet simultaneously. Suddenly, there was a loud cry, followed by another, as the infant shrieked out its presence to the world. All those standing by smiled, laughed and clapped their hands with joy. Kevin quickly removed a shoelace from his sneaker and tied off the umbilical cord, then with the knife, he cut the cord releasing the baby from the afterbirth. A few minutes later, he handed the baby, wrapped in a tablecloth, to the father who knelt beside his wife, tearful with happiness and gratitude.

The sound of the ambulance siren pierced their ears, and moments later the paramedics took charge. Kevin and Africa hugged each other with delight in the way things had turned out. The new father shook their hands profusely, while his wife and infant son were being placed into the ambulance. The quick action of Africa and Kevin had saved the life of the young man in the smaller car. The paramedics, as well as the policeman, and other motorists praised them highly. They were particularly proud of each others performance. All the way to the Hildenbrandt home, they complimented each other as they talked about their experience.

When Kevin stopped the car in front of the house, he told Africa, "Baby, you're all right and I love the sweetest girl in the whole world."

"I love you too, Kevin," she whispered. Their lips met in a kiss that conveyed their love with new meaning.

Together they went directly to Mrs. Hildenbrandt and told of their experience. She was surprised, proud and pleased. Holding both their hands she said to Kevin, "Didn't I tell you, Kevin. She's got what this family needs."

"You're absolutely right, Grandma. She's Number 1 in my book!" Lupe arrived with dinner for Mrs. Hildenbrandt.

"Don't bother to bring Miss Jones' tray, Lupe. She's having dinner with the family, downstairs, tonight," instructed Kevin.

"Oh, no!" exclaimed Africa.

"Oh, yes," insisted Kevin. "Just wash up. I'm going to my room to do the same. I'll be back here for you in three minutes."

Africa looked helplessly at Mrs. Hildenbrandt.

"You heard him. I've got nothing to say," she said smiling and lifting the silver cover on her tray.

Africa washed up, ran a comb through her hair, and refreshed her make up. She was about to change her shorts for a wrap around skirt when Kevin knocked on the door. She opened it, and he insisted on her coming just as she was to dinner.

"You're beautiful and we're late already," he said.

Kevin led Africa into the dining room. Everyone in the family was there and seated with the exception of Gloria Hildenbrandt, Kevin's mother. The men stood as Kevin pulled out a seat next to Jeannie and seated Africa. He then sat next to her. Dr. Hildenbrandt said the blessing, and they all began to eat. Lupe had prepared a delicious dinner. There were collard greens, corn on the cob, scalloped potatoes, ham, salmon croquettes, corn bread, a colorful green salad, enchiladas, freshly baked apple pie for dessert, and fresh, ground, rich coffee.

Jeannie was dressed in a smart, sophisticated after-five dress. She stared at Africa for a moment, then commented, "I see you prefer shorts when not in uniform, Africa. Do you usually dress in that attire for dinner?"

"Not usually," replied Africa.

"Well you ought to," smiled Dr. Hildenbrandt. He chuckled as he continued with, "You're a welcome lift!"

"Agreed," chimed in Mark. "After a long day, you're what we need to rest our eyes in the evening."

"Thank you," replied Africa demurely.

Kevin then began to speak, and he again related their experience of the afternoon. Afterward, Dr. Hildenbrandt and Mark were alive with questions and praise. Even Jeannie took a little interest, and smiled a somewhat reserved smile at Africa before excusing herself earlier than what Africa knew was customary for her.

Mrs. Hildenbrandt never appeared. Her seat remained vacant throughout dinner. Once when Lupe came through the swinging door from the kitchen, Africa glimpsed her there, obviously eating from a plate she held and frowning.

The men toasted Africa and she sipped champagne with them, listening to their anecdotes. Everyone laughed and they had a wonderful time, felt Africa. She had never imagined that they could be so much fun. Dinner came to an end, however, when Kevin had to leave for "on call" duty at the hospital and she returned to Mrs. Hildenbrandt's bedside to prepare her for the night.

CHAPTER 9

raduation day had finally arrived for Africa. Little Joey awakened her early that morning, sitting up in bed, rubbing his eyes, and crying, "Mommie, Mommie!"

Africa glanced at her watch. It was seven thirty. The sun was shining brightly, and she could hear the birds chirping in the orange tree outside the window. She looked over at Brenda's bed. It was empty. As a matter of fact, she thought, it didn't look as if it had been slept in at all. The spread still neatly covered the pillow, and she knew Brenda certainly wouldn't get up and make her bed this early. Joey's shoes were still on the foot of her bed, where they had been when she went to sleep. The child's cries became louder and more persistent. Brenda would never let him cry that long if she

144

were in the house. She was so very devoted to her son.

"O.K., O.K., Baby. Aunt Africa's coming. Don't cry, Joey. It's all right," she crooned and hastened to the crying child. She lifted him from his crib and began to soothe him. Lucy came rushing into the room, obviously upset.

"Good, you've got him. You know, Brenda didn't come home at all last night. I wonder where in the hell she is? I know it's got something to do with that damn Moses. The no good scoundrel. She ain't got a bit of sense! Lord knows, I hope she's all right!"

"O.K., Mama. Stop worrying. She'll be in here in a few minutes. You know she doesn't want Joey to miss her."

"But why couldn't she call?" wailed Lucy.

"Mom! Hey, Mom!" It was Billy in his bare feet and pajama bottoms standing in the middle of the living room. "She's coming, Mom. I just saw Moses let her out of his car. He drove on off."

When the front door opened and Brenda stepped inside, she was verbally blasted by Lucy and Billy.

"You done lost your cotton picking mind," yelled Billy. "Gal, we thought you was dead! That sucker gonna get his neck broke in two!" he

145

finished from his bedroom before slamming the door.

Billy had not finished before Lucy started.

"You're just trying to drive me crazy and kill me, all at the same time!" she cried out at Brenda. "No consideration at all. We got a damn phone, and you know you could have called me. There's no excuse! If you dare to come up here pregnant again, I'm gonna take you and Joey over there on that high falutin job Moses got and leave you both at his window. That's one trip, I'll make. I'll bet you on that! I'll take you bag and baggage! Deed I will."

Joey reached out for Brenda, crying, "Mommie! Mommie!" Africa handed him to Brenda, who seemed not at all affected by the verbal onslaught she had just received. She went into the bedroom without saying a word, closing the door behind her and Joey.

Africa was just so happy to see Brenda safe, that she had nothing to say. Loving Kevin had affected the way she felt towards Brenda and the love she displayed for Moses. Later, while Brenda was bathing Joey, Africa went into the bathroom and told her,

"Next time, Brenda, just call. You know how Mom worries."

It was noon before the household had calmed down again. Lucy told Africa that she definitely would be going to her graduation.

"I'm so proud of you, Honey, you don't know! Brenda and Billy have worked out a plan. They will each stay real close to me and hold my hand all the time. They say I won't have room to feel scared. I'm gonna take one of them tranquilizers the doctor gave me and pray. I'm going, Honey. Your mama will be there to see you graduate. I been looking forward to this all your life. Lord knows, I'm so happy and proud of my baby!" Lucy took her wet hands out of the sink, where she had been washing greens, and hugged Africa close to her bosom.

"Oh, Mom! I'm happy too!" cried Africa.

"Soon as I finish here, I'll start getting ready. I've got to ride with that fool, Moses, but I've made up my mind not to say another word about what happened last night until tomorrow. This is your graduation day, and I want everybody to be happy."

"Good, Mom, that's wonderful," said Africa, as she kissed Lucy, then quickly left the room to dress for her graduation. She had to leave two hours earlier than was necessary for the rest of the family, in order to prepare for the ceremony at the college. Moses had volunteered to take them all in the used

147

Buick he had purchased a few days earlier, thanks to his job at the bank and its credit union.

The graduation was held on the football field at the California State University. Several thousand people were present to observe the awarding of degrees to several hundred deserving young men and women from the University's various departments. Africa's only worry was that Lucy would not be able to tolerate the crowd and either faint or lose control and cry hysterically. The graduation exercise was very well done and beautiful. Africa marched out with her class, each in their white cap and gown and carrying the coveted Bachelor of Science Degree in Nursing diploma, for which they had labored for four long years. She headed for the large palm tree which she and Billy had designated as their meeting place. Approaching through the crowd, she received a shock. There stood Billy and Brenda and squeezed between them was Lucy. Moses held Joey. Next to them was Mrs. Hildenbrandt, her white hair neatly coiffured, dressed in satin and lace and adorned with ropes of precious pearls and fine jewelry. She sat with all the regal bearing of a beautiful queen in her wheelchair. A white clad ambulance attendant stood behind her.

Africa rushed towards them, when suddenly, she collided with an irresistible force. Strong arms encased her, and she looked up into Kevin's smiling face.

"That first congratulatory kiss comes from me," he said. Then his lips sought her's, and his kiss was glorious, effecting her like a glass of the vintage wine. In the excitement she almost lost her cap, and the precious diploma was slightly crumpled as her arms went about his neck. Together they went to join the others. Africa hugged and kissed them all, even Moses. There were tears of happiness in her eyes, as she smiled at both Lucy and Mrs. Hildenbrandt, and accepted all their congratulations.

"I just about exploded when you marched up there and got that diploma," said Lucy.

"Yeah, you was looking good, Africa. Looking good!" exclaimed Moses, with his best grin. Kevin kept his arm about Africa as much as possible and smiled with pleasure each time she accepted a compliment.

"I yelled the loudest when they called your name, Africa. Everybody sitting round us knew you were the greatest. We clapped the longest and the loudest," insisted Billy.

"Well, now that our girl's graduated, let's get this show on the road!" exclaimed Mrs. Hildenbrandt, quite eagerly. "Where's that ambulance man?"

149

"Yeah," said Billy. "Let's go!"

"Mrs. Hildenbrandt's treating us all to dinner, Africa! It's a party for you," explained Brenda with excitement.

They all decided to meet at the Beverly Hilton Hotel where Mrs. Hildenbrandt had arranged the dinner party. Lucy was managing quite well with Billy and Brenda close to her, and each holding her hand. Moses attended to Joey. Africa learned that Kevin had come to the exercises in the ambulance with Mrs. Hildenbrandt, but now, he would remain with Africa, and drive the two of them in the Cadillac to the hotel. They stood watching as the others departed in the crowd. Mrs. Hildenbrandt pushed by the ambulance attendant, and Africa's family as a close little unit sheltering Lucy. Africa knew that without their support the graduation throng would have been devastating to her mother. Kevin and Africa waited for a few moments, then rushed off, hand and hand, happy and laughing, to return her cap and gown, and then rush to the hotel to join the others. At the auditorium, Africa turned in her cap and gown and delighted in introducing Kevin to some of her instructors and classmates. They seemed very much impressed with his congeniality and intelligent good looks. She could tell by a few envious stares, that

150

she was indeed a lucky girl to have him. I hope I have him, she thought smiling to herself.

Africa knew that the dinner party at the Beverly Hilton Hotel was the most fantastic event ever held in her behalf. They served a delicious seven course meal in the most beautiful and lavish surroundings imaginable. Mrs. Hildenbrandt and Kevin seemed right at home in the private dining room. It was obvious that they were accustomed to such opulent extravagance. Both knew the Maitre'd, who made a special effort to see that everything was just perfect. He inquired frequently of Mrs. Hildenbrandt, in his heavy French accent, and engaged in a short, but pleasant conversation with Kevin in French. Africa was seated at the head of the table as guest of honor. She could see herself and the others in the many mirrors, which adorned the walls of the gold and ivory room. She noticed that even little Joey was awed as he sat quietly and stared about himself from the elaborate high chair in which he sat. Africa knew her beige, chiffon dress was perfect. She knew she resembled a princess because she felt like one. Everyone looked either beautiful, romantic or both in this setting, she thought. Even Moses had acquired an aura, and Kevin was the most magnificent man existing.

The expensive wine added to their gaiety. Lucy indulged herself in pleasant sips until she had consumed a full glass with her meal. She accepted another from the formally dressed waiter, who anticipated their slightest needs.

The family, Moses included, presented Africa with a small box, beautifully wrapped in white tissue and tied with a pink bow. She opened it to find the gift she had told Lucy, so many times, she could not afford and would manage to do without. It was her class ring, beautiful in platinum, with a lovely garnet setting, her birthstone. It fit perfectly, and Brenda told her,

"I used one of your old rings for sizing, Africa."

"Thank you! Thank you!" she cried, jumping up from the table and kissing each one of them.

"Come here, Child," commanded Mrs. Hildenbrandt. She gave Africa an envelope, and when Africa opened it, she found a pink slip. "That old Cadillac is now yours," said the old lady. Africa gasped, and then hugged Mrs. Hildenbrandt with joy, until her friend said, "All right, all right, now don't muss my hair all up and choke me to death. I've still got that Blazing Bombay dessert to deal with."

Everybody laughed, and when Africa had again taken her seat, Kevin placed in front of her a small, gold box tied in a red ribbon. Africa nervously opened it and brought forth the most delicate exquisite gold watch she had ever seen. There were small diamonds on either side of the face, set in dainty white gold leaves. She was even more surprised to find that it had a sweep second hand and she could use it on duty. Exclamations arose about the table. Even Joey cried out in response to the others.

"Kevin," she whispered, "It's so beautiful! They just don't make second hands on anything this precious. Oh, Kevin! It's so lovely. I love it!" She leaned over, kissed him, and the effect was intoxicating. Kevin gently fastened the watch, with it's safety catch, on her wrist. The gold dazzled against the brown of her skin. She and Kevin were lost in the beauty of the moment. His deep set, dark eyes reflected love and tenderness, as they met hers, bright with excitement and happiness. Suddenly, the waiter appeared with platters of flame. Little Joey shrieked with excitement as they sliced and served the Flaming Bombay dessert. It was while they were enjoying the delicious ice cream dessert, that Moses rose from his seat and started to speak.

"In spite of the fact that Brenda and I done had all hell raised at us today, I wan...,"

"Aw, Man, sit down," interrupted Billy.

Lucy supported Billy with, "After that caper you pulled last night, you're lucky to be alive to stand."

"Please, stop interrupting!" cried Brenda. "Go on and finish, Moses," she said, nudging his thigh with her elbow.

"Don't worry, I will, but first I want to introduce you to the new Mrs. Moses Brown!"

Brenda jumped up out of her seat, and hugged Moses. Everyone was astonished, as she cried out, "Me and Moses got married last night. This here is my husband!"

"Say what?" yelled Billy, a smile dawning on his face.

"Thank you, Jesus! Lord a Mercy!" cried Lucy.

Africa rushed from her seat to hug them both, and Kevin followed.

"We drove to Las Vegas and was married last night. It was a mad rush, and we were lucky to get back this morning when we did," explained Moses.

Little Joey's eyes were as big as saucers, and he laughed as if he understood what had happened.

" And we owe it all to one hell of a guy. Thank ya, Doc!" exclaimed Moses, as he shook Kevin's hand. "You got me a good job, and now I feel I'm a man, and I can take care of my family."

"You're a good man, Moses. I hear you're doing a great job down at the bank. Congratulations!" said Kevin as he shook Moses' hand. Mrs. Hildenbrandt extended her hand, and congratulated the newlyweds also, as she gave her blessings. The rest of the evening was lively with laughter as Moses teased Lucy and Billy about their treatment of him.

"All's well that ends well," concluded Lucy.

"Well, it's about time for me to go now," said Mrs. Hildenbrandt. "I hate to break up the party, but this is the latest I've been up in six years. What time does that new watch of yours say, Africa?"

"Eleven-ten, Mrs. Hildenbrandt."

Joey had vacated the highchair, and was asleep in Brenda's arms.

"If you all can spare Africa tonight, I'll need her to tuck me in," said the old lady. "I can't remember when I've had such a good time," she continued with a radiant smile.

Kevin sent a waiter for the ambulance attendant, and it took another fifteen minutes for them to thank Mrs. Hildenbrandt, congratulate Africa and the newlyweds, kiss, shake hands, and bid each other good night. Kevin drove Africa to his home. When they arrived the ambulance was leaving.

"She made us turn on the sirens," explained the attendant. "She sure is a card. Most folks are nervous with our driving, but she kept yelling for Ed to floor it!" The fellow laughed, shaking his head as he climbed into the ambulance with the driver and departed.

Africa was in a rush to see to Mrs. Hildenbrandt, but it was difficult to part from Kevin. He held her close to him at the door.

"I've got to go back to the hospital tonight, Sweetheart, but I'll be home Wednesday night. I'm dying to make love to you again. Please don't say, "No." Come to my room at eleven. I know Grandma will be sound asleep by then. Please, think about it."

He kissed her tenderly, and even in her daze Africa responded passionately. He buried his face in her hair, then kissed the lobe of her ear, and that portion of her neck beneath. Africa felt her spine tingle.

"God, Honey, don't say, "No," he whispered, as if in agony and then departed quickly towards his car.

CHAPTER 10

 frica was so happy she felt as if she were floating the next morning as she drove her very own Cadillac home. It seemed to run better than ever, and she didn't see a better looking car on the road. To think that she owned a car, and such a fine one, at this stage in her life was incredible to her. Glancing down at the beautiful watch Kevin had given her was another good feeling. She didn't know anyone who owned such a valuable watch. It sparkled in the sunlight, and the little diamonds constantly winked their brilliance at her. Kevin was so dear, she thought, and she loved him so much. How could she refuse him? But she must, somehow, she must summon the strength. Then she relived his kisses of the night before, and thought, I can't. Dear Lord I do want him as much as he wants me, maybe even more. What can I do? If I lost him, I'd just plain die.   She looked at the lovely graduation ring on her finger. It was beautiful and represented so much, the love and devotion of her family and years of hard work and struggle. To think she was a professional nurse with a college degree. The world had suddenly become her orchard. All she had to do now was to pass the State Board Examination, and obtain her license to practice as a Registered Nurse. Meanwhile, she was fortunate to have such a good job with Mrs. Hildenbrandt. She could study and then sit for the exam next month. Life is indeed beautiful, she thought, as she parked the car in front of her house.

Africa went to church with Billy, Brenda, Moses and Little Joey. They all tried their best to convince Lucy to accompany them, but she maintained that last night had been enough. She would not press her luck. She did agree that attending Africa's graduation and the party was an indication that she must be on the road to recovery, and could possibly overcome her fear of being away from home and in crowds. She promised them that sometime soon, she would go with them to church, and that would be her next excursion.

Later that afternoon, while they were enjoying the delicious dinner she had prepared,

Moses and Brenda informed the family that Brenda would be moving out early in the morning. Lucy had permitted Moses to stay in the house, and he had only spent one night under the roof, sleeping in the room with Brenda and Joey. Africa had noticed, when she arrived that morning, that her bed was completely made up, as if it had not been slept in, while Brenda's was a wreck. She smiled, knowing that Moses was hardly the type to make up his bed, and that Brenda never made up beds early in the morning.

Moses had found a darling little bungalow unit in the complex next to where he had been rooming. It was one of six individual apartments, typical of those found in Los Angeles, each having its own small front and back yard. There were five rooms, which included two bedrooms and one and one half baths. Brenda was thrilled with it, and proud of the fact that Joey could now have his own room, for which she already had exciting plans. Moses said they would live there for a few years until he could save up the down payment to buy their own home. Since it was only four blocks from Lucy's, Brenda would be able to visit every day when she walked Joey.

Lucy was as happy as Brenda. She repeated to her several times, "Now tomorrow, Brenda, early, you call up that Welfare Department. There's the number over there on the coffee table, and you tell them that you're off welfare, that your husband's got a good job, and he's taking care of you and your son. Understand? Now you be sure to do that."

"I can't wait to do it, Mama. I think some of them people thought I'd never get off welfare, but I knew it was just a matter of time."

Brenda was so proud and happy she giggled all during dinner about "everything and nothing" as Billy summed it up. Africa was happy for them too, but she couldn't help but think about what the loss of Brenda's monetary contributions would mean to the household. Well, she would just have to take full responsibility, that's all. Thank the good Lord the house was paid for. She had her job with Mrs. Hildenbrandt who had told her, just this morning, that she would now be paying her a graduate nurse's salary.

Everything is going to work out just beautiful, she told herself, even after Kevin and I are married. Why doesn't he say something? Why hasn't he even mentioned an engagement? I love this watch, but why couldn't it have been an engagement ring? I don't understand. No, I won't go to his room Wednesday, or if I go, I won't make love with him unless he asks me to marry him, or we at least get engaged. He said he loves me but that's not enough. If he loves me, he should want to marry me, make a commitment of some sort. Oh, Lord, help me do the right thing. I love him so. Oh, I love him so much.

"Africa, are you all right? What's wrong with you, Girl" asked Billy.

"You look like you just dropped off the world there," agreed Brenda.

"I'm fine. I was just thinking about how much we'll all miss you and Joey, Brenda. But I'm so happy about everything that's happening for you and Moses."

Africa thought a great deal the next two days, and asked herself the same questions over and over again, but with only temporary resolutions. She now spent all day with Mrs. Hildenbrandt, but kept her books near and studied at every opportunity possible, in preparation for her Registered Nurse State Board Examination.

They had not long finished dinner, and Mrs. Hildenbrandt was watching television news. Africa was curled up in the comfortable Queen Anne's chair next to her bed, studying, when Kevin appeared. As usual he kissed his grandmother, and greeted Africa with a warm, handsome smile. He took a seat on the other side of Mrs. Hildenbrandt's bed and patted her hand affectionately. Together, they watched the remainder of the news, and a detective story. Africa and Kevin stole frequent highly charged glances at one another, while laughing or commenting with Mrs. Hildenbrandt on the program.

"Well, it's my bedtime now," said the old lady at the conclusion of the program. I'm unusually tired tonight. Children, I feel like I could sleep forever."

Kevin bade her a loving good-night, and squeezed Africa's hand, giving her a wistful look, with a special smile as he left the room.

"I can't help feeling there's something special going on between you and Kevin, Africa. He loves you very much, I can tell, and you love him too, don't you?"

"Mrs. Hildenbrandt, you know, I just can't believe it's possible to love anyone as much as I love Kevin."

"Then the two of you need to get married. The quicker the better. You're right for each other, and you're the two young people I love most. Don't get me wrong now, I love Mark, too, but there's just something special between Kevin and me. He's always been so wonderful to his grandmother, and I'm grateful."

"I understand, Mrs. Hildenbrandt. Kevin told me he loved me, so maybe soon, he'll ask me to marry him."

"He will, Dear. He will. Kevin has always been one to think things out. He knows how I feel about the two of you, and that I know you'd be the best thing ever happened to this family. Gloria will come around after awhile. I don't know how she got so snooty. Maybe it's because she never had change in clothes until she married my son. It has just all gone to her head," sighed Mrs. Hildenbrandt, as she applied her night cream.

Africa made her comfortable and watched her drop off to sleep, as she tidied up the room. Mrs. Hildenbrandt was snoring when she went into the sitting room.

I'm not going, thought Africa, as she ran her bath water and sprinkled in her favorite bath oil. She took a comfortable bath, then stepped out onto the soft pink carpeting to pat herself dry. Noticing her body in the full length door mirror, she remembered the passion she had felt at Kevin's pleasure in viewing and touching her.

I'm not going, she thought again, as she slipped into her most beautiful gown of peach satin and ivory lace. Usually she would brush and pin her thick hair into a bun for sleeping, but tonight, she

163

combed and brushed her wavy mane until it shone luxuriously, and fell softly about her shoulders. Africa looked at the clock, as she pulled the covers over her, and lie quietly in bed. It was eleven fifty-five. Good, she thought, now he knows I'm not coming. But what if he wanted to ask me to marry him tonight? If I don't go, I'll never know.

Kevin's room was the only one to the right , at the top of the stairs. Africa gave three light raps on the door, which was immediately opened by Kevin. He was heartbreakingly handsome in a maroon, silk dressing coat over his pajamas. He said not a word, but the smile on his face told her how happy he was to see her. Quickly, but gently he pulled her inside the room and into his arms.

"Africa! Baby, I had just about given up on you," he whispered into her hair. She clung to him, feeling her resistance melting into anticipation.

"Kevin, I was thinking," she whispered. Their hearts seemed to beat as one, with an ever increasing tempo.

"Don't," he said, interrupting, then kissing her tenderly. Their passion mounted, and his kisses became more earnest as she returned them with a fervor indicating her desire to be as great as his.

In spite of the overwhelming longing which swelled within her, Africa was able to muster the strength for a final attempt to uphold her principles. Her sudden struggle disarmed Kevin as she pulled away from him.

"Honey, what's wrong?" he asked. And in the soft light from the lamp on his bedside table, she could see his expression of bewilderment.

"We've got to talk, Kevin," she said softly. Her bright eyes were beautiful and pleading as she retreated from him. She felt weak and lonely. For the first time she looked about. Her eyes swept quickly over the room taking in the beauty of its fine masculine furnishings, which included a massive four poster, mahogany, king sized bed, matching chiffonier and dresser. There was also a desk, and wall of bookcases, which housed a fine stereo component, as well as books. An exquisite red and blue Persian rug with an intricate design, covered the large floor area. The bathroom door was ajar and she noted its blue and red marble. The room was in perfect accord with Kevin, the rest of the house, and the finery she had expected. Africa seemed to collapse into the big, comfortable armchair behind her.

Kevin looked down at her.

"Kevin, where are we going? We just can't continue like this. I'm afraid. Maybe you really don't love me."

A softness and tenderness now replaced the bewilderment on Kevin's fine features. He reached for her hands, and bending, kissed them before pulling her to her feet. His eyes held hers with sincerity and he seemed to look deeply inside her soul, as he spoke.

"Africa, my love, there is no need to say more. I know exactly where you're coming from. Please, trust me. You've got to trust me, Honey. God knows I love you with all my heart. I need you."

His strong arms engulfed her, and Africa knew then, that she would never ever be able to resist Kevin again.

He seemed to have kissed away her peignoir and gown. When he lifted her onto his king sized bed , she floated between its water mattress and the strength of his magnificent body. A sweet passion raged within her as he murmured tones and phrases of endearment, with appreciation of her beauty. His hands tenderly caressed and explored her body while their kisses ignited flames of desire. She clung to him as if he were life itself, as she experienced an unbelievable ecstasy, the throes of which transported her away from earth and into a heavenly bliss. Their love making seemed endless, and their thirst for each other was unsatiable. An unquenchable fire raged out of control, and with their satisfaction, merely pacified, they slept from pure exhaustion, entwined lovingly in each others arms.

Africa awakened to Kevin's kisses, and immediately responded, eager to resume their love making. Kevin's soft laughter emerged between their kisses.

"Honey, it's almost morning. I hate to say it, Baby, but you've got to split."

Africa was shocked at the time, but was in reluctant agreement. Their laughter was mirthful as she struggled to climb out of his floating, rollicking bed. Kevin watched dreamily as she hastily pulled on her gown and peignoir. At the door, they shared a final kiss of love, before she slipped into the hallway.

As Africa rushed towards her room, she was startled to catch a glimpse of a woman, in a white robe, staring at her from the shadows, barely reached by the hallway's dim light. The woman stood a short distance from Dr. and Mrs. Hildenbrandt's master suite. When she turned and departed towards that suite, Africa recognized her as Gloria, Kevin's mother, and knew then that she was aware of hers and Kevin's love tryst.

Africa was snug in her bed, sleepily savoring the thrills and pleasure of the time she had spent with Kevin. The uneasiness she felt because of Gloria Hildenbrandt's knowledge of her visit to Kevin's room was minimized in her happiness. Suddenly, she became aware that all was not right. She sprung from her bed, and to the older Mrs. Hildenbrandt's door. There was no sound of her patient's stertorous breathing. She quickly flipped on the room's overhead light, and rushed to Mrs. Hildenbrandt's bedside. Panic seized her as she stared at the woman, because at one glance, she knew Mrs. Hildenbrandt was dead. Her eyes were open, and staring, and her mouth open and still.

Africa moved swiftly, but as an automan, as she yanked on the bed side cord, which sent the sound of chimes ringing urgently throughout the big house. She fastened her mouth over the cold morbid one, and squeezing the nose with her hand, began the act of cardio-pulmonary resuscitation, blowing her breath into Mrs. Hildenbrandt's non-functioning lungs. Kevin and his father reached her simultaneously. It was Kevin who took her away from the body, as his father ceased his efforts at chest compression.

"It's no point, Dad," she heard Kevin say. "Rigor Mortis has even set in."

"You're right, Son."

There was the piercing sound of screams, followed by sobs. Africa saw Mark attempt to comfort Jeannie, as he led her from the room, sobbing himself. Lupe was wringing her hands, and crying while Jose muttered a prayer. They left the room together with silent tears of sadness. Gloria Hildenbrandt stood at her husband's side, as he stood looking in grief at his dead mother. She glared angrily across the body at Africa, whom Kevin held in his arms. Africa lowered her eyes so she would not have to meet Gloria's accusing ones. Her cheeks were stained with tears, and she felt the sadness in Kevin as he struggled for control.

"I'm going to call the undertaker," he said finally. Releasing Africa he left the room. Dr. Hildenbrandt had closed his mother's eyes, after a final examination with the stethoscope from the dresser. He covered her completely with the bed sheet.

"My God," he whispered in dismay, "She's gone. Gloria, she's gone. I'll have to go with Kevin and help make arrangements. Come, Dear." His shoulders were bent and he appeared broken, as he left the room to catch Kevin. He was well out the door before Gloria made any attempt to follow. She moved close to Africa, who seemed glued to her spot. Africa gasped as the woman's hand reached out and struck her a stinging blow across her cheek.

"You little whore! You should have been with her! Pack your things and leave this house immediately. That old Cadillac and your paycheck will be the last things you'll take from here!" Gloria quickly ran from the room to join her husband. Africa did as she was ordered. Jose brought her check to the room as she packed. Kevin was nowhere in sight when she left the house, carrying her bags. Minutes later, she drove, facing the rising sun, down the driveway, headed home.

CHAPTER 11

Lucy was saddened to hear of Mrs. Hildenbrandt's demise. She attempted to comfort her daughter, who took the old lady's death very hard. Africa spent the whole day in bed. She refused to eat, and would begin crying whenever Lucy attempted to console her or mention Mrs. Hildenbrandt's name. Africa dared not mention the details of her patient's death to her mother.

Kevin called Africa the next morning. She was overjoyed to hear from him.

"Look, Sweetheart, I can't talk very long. I'm up to my neck here at the hospital, but I just want you to know there will be a quick funeral. That's what Grandma wanted. It'll be tomorrow at two o'clock at the First Baptist Church over on Adams."

"Oh, Kevin, I'm so sorry. I feel so guilty."

"Don't you dare! We need to talk, Darling. I wanted to see you again yesterday, but you left so soon. I'll look forward to seeing you tomorrow, Honey. I've got to run now. I'm between an appendectomy and a herniaorraphy. Love ya, doll and I'm missing you every minute."

"Me too, Kevin. I love you too."

There was the sound of a big kiss from the other end of the line and Kevin saying, "Bye, Love." Then a click up.

Africa was unable to convince Lucy that she could attend Mrs. Hildenbrandt's funeral.

"I hate funeral's, Africa. You know that. I don't want to push my luck, leaving home. You just give my condolences to the family and I'll send a nice card."

The First Baptist Church was packed. The Hildenbrandt family was highly respected and very well known in the city. Mrs. Hildenbrandt, her late husband, and their Savings and Loan Institution, as well as Insurance Company, had become tradition as well as history to Los Angeles. Old time friends came to pay their respects to the family's matriarch, and wife of the companies' founder. Africa was ushered to a seat in the balcony of the church, and considered herself fortunate, since many mourners were left standing on the sidewalk.

When Africa's turn arrived to file by the casket, and view Mrs. Hildenbrandt's remains, she felt extremely weak. Looking momentarily at her old friend, lying peaceful, and resembling a beautiful queen at rest, seemingly transfused her with renewed energy, and she was able to continue on with the other viewers and pass down the aisle. She noticed the family sitting on the front row. Her eyes met Kevin's and he gave her a sweet and secret smile. Dr. Hildenbrandt had his head bowed, as did Mark. She did not look at the women, however, she could not help but notice Nanette, who was seated directly behind Kevin.

Africa drove alone in the funeral procession to the cemetery. Lupe and Jose greeted her, and stood by her side in the crowd as the minister spoke his final words, and their former employer's casket was lowered into its grave. Afterwards, Africa joined the line which filed by the grieving family members to shake their hands and offer condolences. Dr. Hildenbrandt shook hands with her warmly, as did Mark. Gloria Hildenbrandt and Jeannie ignored her, and she did not make any effort to attract their attention. Kevin held both her hands for a long moment. His eyes were sad, as his gaze met hers, but she could not miss the gratefulness and love he directed to her. Neither spoke, and he released her to accept the next outstretched hand and words of sympathy.

Africa waited until the family arose to leave. She started towards Kevin, but stopped when she noticed Nanette holding his arm. He and the other family members walked to the waiting limousines. Jose drove one, and assisted Lupe into the seat next to him. Africa pressed closer, but was stopped by Gloria Hildenbrandt's cold, warning stare, as she beckoned to Kevin and Nanette to join her and Dr. Hildenbrandt in the waiting limousine. Kevin's head was lowered, in grief, and she knew that he did not see her.

Africa stood on the mossy, green grass, her high, black heels sinking into the soft earth, and watched the limousines carrying her lover, his family and Nanette down the winding road, and out of the cemetery.

It was three days after the funeral, and Africa had not heard any word from Kevin. On the fourth day, she became quite ill, and remained in bed most of the day. After one week, and still no word, she went to the hospital to see Kevin. She was shocked when told by the Chief of Surgery, that

Kevin was no longer a resident physician at the hospital, and that he had completed his training there. Africa drove quickly back home and called the Hildenbrandt house. Lupe informed her that Kevin was not in, and that he was out of town. She also said that she could not give any further information, as Mrs. Hildenbrandt had directed her not to tell Africa anything about Kevin, if she were to call. Actually she was not to have spoken to her at all, but was to have hung up the phone immediately as soon as she heard her voice.

Africa left home immediately after talking with Lupe, and drove to the Hildenbrandt home. Still in possession of the main gate key, she was able to drive up in front of the house without asking to be admitted. She alighted from the Cadillac to see Jose placing luggage into the family's new Rolls Royce. Africa rushed past the handyman with a quick, "Hi, Jose," in response to his friendly greeting. Just as she entered the foyer, whose door was open wide, she met Nanette and Mrs. Hildenbrandt, smartly dressed in traveling suits, leaving the house.

"What is this?" asked Nanette with disdain, as she stared at Africa, who ignored her, and approached Mrs. Hildenbrandt.

"I want to see Kevin," she said to his mother.

"Well. he doesn't wish to see you!" retorted Gloria Hildenbrandt.

"Where is he?" cried Africa in distress.

"None of your business!" yelled Nanette.

"It is my business!" screamed Africa back at Nanette. "He loves me, and I love him. He's all my business, and I want to know where he is!"

"You little fool!" laughed Nanette.

"Quiet, Nanette. I'll handle this," said Gloria. "Come with me, Africa. I want to settle this once and for all." She started towards the study.

"Mrs. Hildenbrandt, we don't have time to waste with this stupid ass. We'll miss our plane, and she's not worth that!" insisted Nanette. Africa followed Mrs. Hildenbrandt, who yelled impatiently to Nanette. "I told you to be quiet. I know what I'm doing. Now, get in the car!"

Inside the study, Gloria Hildenbrandt shut the door after Africa.

Africa remembered the last time she and Kevin had been in the study together, as she demanded of his mother, "Where is Kevin?' "He is not here," said Gloria Hildenbrandt, as she studied Africa.

"I know that. Where is he?"

"I'm not going to tell you where he is, because he does not want me to."

"What do you mean?" asked Africa, tears welling in her eyes.

"I almost feel sorry for you, Girl, but you should have known better. Kevin is in the south, He has left California for a new life. Nanette and I are going there now. She and Kevin will be married as soon as we arrive."

"You're lying! Kevin wouldn't marry her. He loves me!"

"You silly, little thing. What would Kevin want with you? Who are you? Nobody! You have nothing to offer him. Nanette has everything, beauty, family, money, background, education, personality, and social position. I could go on and on. You've nothing but your looks, and a degree to work! Nanette's got that and so much more. How did you ever expect to compete with her? Oh, but you're stupid!" cried Gloria, shaking her head in disgust.

"That's you, not Kevin. He doesn't feel that way. He loves me."

"He used you! He had to! Why do you think he went away and left you. Did he tell you he was leaving? Of course not. I know he didn't because he doesn't need you anymore. Momma Hildenbrandt was senile. You took advantage of her!"

"That's a lie!" cried Africa.

"You took advantage of her," repeated Gloria Hildenbrandt. "We all knew she was crazy and wanted Kevin to marry you, so he agreed to play a part. She threatened once to put us all out and sell this house. She could have done it. Everything was hers, the company, money, house, everything. She controlled it all and to save us, Kevin tried to please her. Nanette even agreed to go along with it. Now, she's gone, we've all got what belongs to us, and Kevin is free, free to marry Nanette, and not have to bother with you, ever again. Now do you understand?"

Africa stared at her, an incredulous expression on her beautiful face, unable to speak. There was the sound of a honking horn.

"I must go. Please leave. Now you know the truth," said Mrs. Hildenbrandt as she turned towards the door.

"Just one minute, Mrs. Hildenbrandt. I owe you something," said Africa. Her voice was steady and calm. Reaching out she mustered all her strength and slapped Mrs. Hildenbrandt hard across the cheek. The woman reeled, and fell against the wall. Shock and fear registered in her eyes, as she

178

struggled to regain her balance, and placed her hand to her face. Africa opened the door, and immediately left the study. She could hear Gloria Hildenbrandt running after her screaming,

"Police! Call the police!"

Nanette and Jose jumped out of the car, and rushed towards Mrs. Hildenbrandt.

"Anything she tells you is a lie," Africa said to Jose as she passed him. Minutes later, she was on the freeway, and again headed homeward. From her window, she dropped the keys to the main gate.

CHAPTER 12

frica felt horrible. She had the feeling that she had been physically beaten. Her body ached, and there was a terrible taste in her mouth that water did not take away.

Kevin, my dearest Kevin, was it true? How could you do this to me? You love me. I know it. How can I believe anything else after all we've meant to each other, the love we've shared? These thoughts turned over and over in her mind. She could see his eyes, pleading her to trust him. She felt his arms about her, his kisses on her mouth, the pleasure he expressed in his whispered words of love to her, and his sighs and moans of rapture as they made love. Kevin, Kevin! It can't be true! I'll never believe in anything again. I'll never love anyone, the way I love you. It can't be true, yet, it had been over a week, and she had not heard from him. He finished his residency at the hospital without telling her, and left town without a word. Oh, God, what was the reason? The loss of her dear friend, Mrs. Hildenbrandt was painful enough, but now the prospect that she had lost Kevin too, was more than she could bear. She also needed a job. The telephone was shut off for non payment, and she didn't want Billy to quit school. Africa also had another problem. She wept softly, tossed and turned, moaning about her problems until she finally became exhausted, and fell into a sound sleep.

Lucy said to Africa that she must have a virus, but Africa gave her another diagnosis.

"I'm pregnant, Mom."

"Oh, no, Africa! Oh, no! Tell me you're joking. Tell me it's not true! It's got to be the flu, pneumonia, anything, but not pregnancy."

"I can't. Mom. I'm a week late, and I know."

"Oh, dear God, how did this happen?" screamed Lucy.

"Easy, Mom. We only made love twice, and it happened the first time."

"Didn't my warnings mean anything to you? I told you and told you!"

"What the devil's going on in here?" asked Billy, rushing through the bedroom door in his pants and undershirt.

"Nothing," said Africa.

"What the hell you mean, nothing. You both look like you're dead, and Mom's screaming at the top of her lungs." Lucy seemed to have regained some composure.

"Africa thinks she's contracted TB," she said sadly.

"What?" asked Billy in dismay.

"Oh, stop it, both of you," said Africa, getting out of bed.

"I'll go to a doctor, and check it out today. I can't be sure without an x-ray."

"Well, I hope not," said Billy. "Didn't they feed you, or let you get any rest over there at the Hildenbrandts'? Sometimes rich folks is stingy as hell! I hope you don't know as much as you think you do, and you're all wrong, Africa. Maybe you ought to give up nursing," said Billy as he left the room. Africa shut the door after him, then began to pick out her clothing for dressing.

"When are you and Kevin getting married, Africa?" asked Lucy.

Africa then told her what had transpired since Mrs. Hildenbrandt's funeral.

"It's early, Africa. You can have an abortion, if it's true."

"I don't believe in abortions, Mom. I feel about that the same as you and Brenda. Besides, I still love Kevin. I could never kill the fruit of our love."

"Don't talk crazy," said Lucy.

"I've got a profession, Mom. I can work and take care of myself and the baby."

"Shit! This place is just one damn mess after the other. I think one problem is solved, and here's another. Chuck Wilson called from up there at the sanitarium yesterday. He said he read about Mrs. Hildenbrandt's death and knew you would be out of a job. Said he would hire you back as evening nursing supervisor at a top salary. I told you'd start Monday."

"No you didn't."

"Yes I did, and you will. You need a job. We need the money and now you need a husband."

"No, Mom. Now you've really got it wrong," said Africa as she yanked on her robe.

There was a loud knocking at the door, then Billy's voice, "Mom! You better get the hell out'ta there until Africa finds out. I'm on my way to school now, but I'll be anxious to know what that doctor says, soon as I get home tonight."

183

They heard the front door slam.

"I'm going to have to talk to that boy. I damn sure don't like his cursing, and Lord knows, I've done my best to teach him better. Must be the crowd he runs with," sighed Lucy. "Now, I'll be waiting to hear too, Africa. I know you're going to have a pregnancy test."

"Waste of time, but I'll do it," said Africa as she opened the door, and proceeded down the hall to the bathroom.

Africa worked two weeks at New Hope before she received her first pay check with only one week's pay. It would be enough to turn the telephone back on and pay a few bills. She hated coming back but loved her work. Ms. Thornton was still the Director of Nursing, but since Africa worked evenings, and was now her evening supervisor, she made some effort at treating the girl in a civil manner. Africa made certain she was always early for work, and of course this pleased the woman, because she was able to leave a few minutes early. Nurses and former patients alike were happy to see Africa, and even arranged a welcoming party for her one afternoon. She knew Chuck was pleased to have her, because the last evening supervisor had quit for an easier acute hospital position, where she wouldn't have to render nursing care, and do administrative work at the same time.

Chuck greeted Africa in a friendly manner, and since he usually left for the day, an hour after she came on duty, she was able to avoid too much contact with him. She decided that Lucy had obviously settled a great deal regarding her future with the sanitarium, during the earlier telephone conversation, which resulted in her being rehired. Chuck Wilson did however, ask two questions, which seemed very important to him, and they were, what had happened between Kevin and her, and would she still consider becoming his, Chuck's, wife? The former, she declined to answer, by saying it was very personal, and she did not wish to discuss it at that time. He answered the question for her the following week, when she arrived on duty. He asked her into his office, whereupon her arrival, he presented her with the society section of the Los Angeles Tribune. He then pointed out an announcement which stunned her to the point of weakness. There was a big, beautiful picture of Nanette, over which was the caption.

"Local Socialite to Wed."

Under the picture were the details of the engagement announcement which began with, 'Mr. and Mrs. Leo Lee, publishers of the Los Angeles

Tribune, take great pleasure in announcing the engagement of their daughter, Miss Nanette Kay Lee, to Dr. Kevin Douglas Hildenbrandt, son of Dr. and Mrs. Samuel Hildenbrandt, and grandson of the late Mr. and Mrs. Wiley L. Hildenbrandt, founders of the Quality Mutual Savings and Loan Institution and the South Western Mutual Insurance Company." The article continued giving facts and dates.

Africa fought for composure, as Chuck said, "I see you were jilted."

She did not answer him, as she placed the paper on his desk, and turned to leave. He caught her by the arm.

"You're still the most beautiful girl I know, Africa, and I'm waiting." At this time she answered his second question asked on her first day back at work.

"I do not plan, ever, to marry anyone, Chuck," and left the office.

When Africa arrived home that night, Lucy was waiting with the newspaper. Africa explained to her how she had already seen the announcement, and related her conversation regarding marriage with Chuck Wilson.

"Africa, don't be no fool. Tell him, yes. You can go to Las Vegas and be married this weekend.

186

He'll never know the difference, when you have the baby. Most babies come early these days anyway. You can work there with him or stay home and raise a family and have everything you've ever wanted."

"Everything but love, Mom. I don't love Chuck. I couldn't do it! Don't you understand that?"

"No, I don't. All I understand is that you're crazy as a loon," and with that Lucy angrily left the kitchen, slamming the door behind her.

Africa sat at the kitchen table for a few minutes drinking a glass of warm milk. I'm surprised they aren't already married, she thought. I guess they decided to postpone it for a big bash. The article did say it would take place in a few weeks. Kevin, how could you, and not one word to me? Certainly I deserved that much. The devastation and loneliness she felt was like none she had ever known. Africa silently cried herself to sleep that night. She decided Kevin would never know about their child. Her pregnancy test had been positive.

Payday proved to be somewhat stressful. Billy was to come pick up Africa's check, then rush to the telephone company, and have the phone service turned on again. However, Chuck, Africa concluded had decided to play games. He was not at the sanitarium when she arrived, however, he had left everyone's check for her to pass out but kept hers. The secretary said he had left word that he would return with Africa's later. Billy didn't like Chuck anyway, and when he arrived, and heard the story, he was not at all happy, to say the least. It was Friday, and he wanted the telephone on for the week end so that he might receive a few important calls from his coach, whom he had assured it would be all right to call him Friday or Saturday. Now there would be no phone for the weekend. Africa tried to make it up to him by letting him take the Cadillac and drive over to his coach's house to wait for him and receive the messages. It was ten o'clock when Billy called her to say that on the way back from his coach's house he had run out of gas, and had to leave the car parked and walk home. He was calling from the drugstore on the corner just before starting his hike. Earlier, he had been over to try and borrow from Brenda and Moses, but they were out.

"That damned Chuck is responsible for all of this," he told Africa.

"Now, he's messing up with me! I'll walk up to meet you at eleven, Africa, just like before."

When Billy arrived home, he found Lucy depressed. She gave him supper, but had little to say.

"What's eating you, Mom?"

"Africa, Billy."

"Well, she said the x-ray was O.K.,, and she doesn't have TB, so what's to worry about now?"

"You might as well know now, Son. It's gonna come out soon, so you might as well know."

"Know what?" Billy asked with alarmed curiosity.

"Africa's pregnant."

"Damn! What the hell's going down around here! First Brenda, and now Africa. Look like there ain't no respect. Shit! I'm the man of this house, and I'm tired of these low down bastards coming round here messing up my sisters."

"Now, don't get excited, Billy," said Lucy, as she reached out to comfort him.

""You've got to stop all this cursing, and watch your English."

"Sorry Mom, but do you know what you just laid on me? I'm upset, and I mean I'm real upset!"

"It's no reflection on you, Baby. It happens in the best of families. My daddy was right there, and it happened to me, too."

Billy stared at his mother.

"What you mean it happened to you, too? You ain't got no illegitimate children." He looked at her again. "Or do you?"

Lucy only looked back at her son.

"Well, I know I'm not, cause I'm the youngest, and Africa's the spitting image of Dad, and Brenda....," he stopped, thinking.

"Brenda, Mom?" he asked.

"She was adopted by your father, Son."

Billy leaned against the sink, and covered his face with both hands for a moment.

"You women are too much for me, Mom. I swear to hell! Poor Brenda. Does she know?"

"Yes."

"Africa know?"

"Yes."

"Damn, Mom! Everybody knew but me. Now that's what I mean, no respect! Poor Africa," he continued. "When's she getting married?"

Lucy was silent. She turned to leave the kitchen.

"Mom!" Billy yelled. "The bottom line here is that Africa ain't married. Now, I want to know when it's gonna happen and who's the Dude?"

"She and that Chuck Wilson just ought'a get married," said Lucy as she left the kitchen.

"They will," muttered Billy after she had gone. He glanced at his watch, walked over to the refrigerator, and taking the pistol from off the top, he put it into his pocket.

"Brenda adopted! My half sister. Africa knocked up. Oh, man, this is heavy. Talk about disrespect, well damn it, I gotta do something about this," he continued to mutter, as he rushed out the back door, slamming it hard behind him.

Lucy heard Billy slam the back door. She sat in front of the television, thinking and not seeing any of the program on it's screen.

If Africa's gonna marry that Chuck Wilson, she better hurry up and do it, she thought. At this point she won't have any explaining to do when the baby's born, but in another week or so she'll be burnt up. Poor Billy. Such a shame I had to tell him about Brenda like that. Poor boy, I wonder..."

Lucy suddenly jumped to her feet, and ran to the kitchen. She felt on top the refrigerator for the gun. It was gone. Of course he would take it with him, but could he have gone after Chuck? She remembered her statement to him, that Africa and Chuck should get married. She hadn't meant that Chuck was the father, she was only expressing her true feelings without answering Billy's question. But what if he had interpreted it differently? Forgetting everything else, she ran out the back door.

CHAPTER 13

huck Wilson arrived just as Africa was going off duty. He met her in the hospital's foyer.

"I've got something for you," he said, holding a brown envelope, which she knew contained her pay check, out to her. He was dressed in a pinstriped, navy blue suit and looked very neat. She became aware that he had even lost a few pounds.

"Thank you. Better late than never. Why do I rate such special attention?'

"Because you're a very special person. Africa, let me drive you home. I held your check, so I would have an excuse for coming back late. I was here earlier, but when I saw you didn't have your car, I decided to wait and come back now, hoping you'd let me take you home."

"My brother, Billy, is coming for me."

"Well, it's after eleven, and he's not here yet. Come on, give me a break. He probably overslept and I'll have you home in no time."

Africa thought for a second. Billy may well have fallen asleep, because when he used to meet her, he was always early, and he had been out of the routine for sometime. What harm could it do.

"O.K., Chuck. Thank you."

He smiled gratefully, and opened the heavy entrance door for her. Chuck had seated Africa and was just about to enter his car from the driver's side, when he looked up to see Billy running towards them. Billy approached calling Chuck's name. Chuck was shocked when he saw that Billy was pointing a pistol at him.

"What is this, Kid?" he asked, staring down the barrel from across the car's engine.

Africa yelled, "Billy! Billy! Have you gone crazy?"

"Hush, Sis, or I'll kill him right here and now," answered Billy into the window Africa had lowered. He held the gun with both hands.

"Look, Man," he said to Chuck. "I'm tired of your messing round with my sister. I don't want no more shit, Nigger. Now, you get in this car, and next time I see the two of you, she better be Mrs. Wilson, or I'll pepper your ass with every damn bullet in this pistol. Hear me?"

"Why of course, Billy. No need to get so worked up. I been trying."

"You damn right you been trying. Now you just consider this a shotgun. I don't play. I'm the man of the house and I say you gonna have a shotgun wedding. Now, get going."

"Yes Sir, Billy. Don't worry. It's as good as done," answered Chuck. Wasting no time, he quickly jumped into the car, and drove off with a roar.

Africa was stunned. They hadn't gone a block when Chuck stopped to let a pedestrian rush by, in the crosswalk. Africa screamed, "Mom!"

Lucy paused on the other side of the street, after crossing. Chuck sped off again in a fury.

What did you do that for?" cried Africa. "That was my mother."

"Don't you think I know it! She might have a pistol too, and I ain't taking no chances."

"Don't be ridiculous! Go back. She's out alone, and she has agoraphobia! Somebody's got to be with her!"

"Well, it won't be either of us cause she's liable to be packing, too, and I got pistolphobia."

"You just passed my street. Where are you taking me?"

"Just down the road here a piece," he answered. Africa heard a click, as he locked the windows and doors from the master control on his side of the car. Chuck drove into a secluded park and brought the Cadillac to a halt on the far side of a baseball diamond under a tree. It was quite dark and lonely. Africa could see that no one was around. Chuck shut off the engine and the lights.

"You heard what your brother said, didn't you?"

"He doesn't understand, Chuck. I'm not going to marry you."

"Oh, yes you will," he said moving closer to her. "I'll bet you'll marry me if I get you pregnant, and that's just what I intend to do."

"You can't," said Africa, she was both dismayed and frightened

"Don't underestimate me, Gal. There ain't nothing wrong with me, and this front seat's got all the room I need."

Reaching out, he grabbed Africa, and held her to him. His lips covered hers in a wet, rough kiss. She struggled against him, but his strength was so great that she could hardly move. She began to feel nauseated and weak. Africa realized that she was no match for Chuck, and her struggling was in vain. He was roughly pushing her head back against the door handle.

"O.K., Chuck, O.K.," she said to him in a whimpering voice, "You win. Let me up. There's no need to fight about this. That way neither of us can have any pleasure. It really shouldn't be that way." Slowly, he relaxed his hold on her, and she began to tenderly stroke his face.

"You've loved me all the time, Africa, haven't you?" he asked, his breathing increasing noticeably.

"Yes, I guess I have, Chuck." She kissed him again. He placed one hand over her breast and the other rubbed her thighs under her skirt.

"Chuck, Darling, please let's get in the back seat. I'm uncomfortable here. Please. I want you to make love to me, Darling, but let's be comfortable, so that we can enjoy it."

O.K., Baby," he said quickly. His physical response was so fast, that it surprised Africa. In seconds, she heard the car latch release the doors, and he was outside the car. Before he could reach her side of the car, Africa had opened her door, and was running in the darkness. She could hear Chuck cursing as he followed behind her.

Africa was not familiar with the park, and was attempting to find the quickest way to the main street. She reached a pathway leading towards a road with lights, and could tell that Chuck was gaining on her.

"You little Bitch," he called, "I was a fool for trusting you. Just wait till I catch you!"

Africa stumbled and almost fell. She was able to break her fall by thrusting both hands onto a tree, but she ended up on her knees. She lost a second or two by getting to her feet, and regaining her balance. Chuck's running feet sounded closer, and she became terrified at the prospect of his getting his hands on her again, because she was now aware that he was angry as well as frantic. In case he did catch up with her, and it seemed that he would any second, Africa decided to play her trump card.

"You can't get me pregnant, Chuck! I'm already pregnant. I'm pregnant already, do you hear? I'm already pregnant!" Suddenly, Africa met an immovable force and strong arms enveloped her. She was near a park lantern, which illuminated the face before her. It was Kevin. Africa went limp in Kevin's arms and all she could manage was to whisper his name over and over, breathlessly.

"It's all right, Honey. It's me, Sweetheart. It's Kevin, all right." A second or two later, Chuck skidded to a breathless halt and confronted them.

O.K., Joker! What's this all about?" demanded Kevin, releasing Africa, and taking a defiant position in front of her.

"What's it to you? Move! Clear out!" yelled Chuck, reaching out to push Kevin aside.

Kevin reacted quickly with a hard right to Chuck's jaw, a left to his middle, and another right to his head. The three blows came in such rapid succession that Chuck didn't have a chance. With each one he retreated backward and downward, ending in a relaxed sprawl, outstretched on the pavement. Kevin paused, leaning over his form for a second, reached down and felt his pulse, after which he told Africa,

"He'll be all right. Just knocked the rest of the wind out of him. Come on, Honey," he said to Africa, as he put his arms about her and led the way to his car. Once inside, Africa broke down in tears of happiness as she and Kevin kissed and held one another as if it were their last chance at loving each other.

"Oh, Kevin, I'm so happy to see you. How did you find me? It was just in time. I was losing out to Chuck, but fast."

"So, I noticed. I met your brother and your mother up at New Hope. They were standing outside, engaged in some sort of a very animated conversation, when I drove up. I asked for you and they told me you had just driven off with this Wilson guy. Your mother said I'd better catch you quick, because you had been kidnapped. They described the car for me, and I took off. Luckily, I spotted his car and followed it here. Actually, I lost him for a few minutes, but remembered passing this park and decided to double back and check it out. Good thing I did." Kevin hugged her tightly as he continued, "Baby, this is one time I'm thankful for the right hunch."

"Thank God, Kevin," whispered Africa.

"Honey, didn't I tell you to trust me? We've got a lot of talking to do but what's this I heard you telling that clown back there about you already being pregnant? I gathered his intentions. Tell me, Africa, are you really pregnant?"

"It's true, Kevin. We're going to have a baby," she said. He held her close to him for a long moment, then released her and started the engine. Africa was anxious for his response to her announcement, but didn't expect this reaction.

"Where are we going, Kevin? Are you angry?"

With a chuckle he answered, "We are on our way to Las Vegas to get married, Honey. That's what I had planned for us anyway."

"But, Kevin, look at me. I'm still in uniform."

"Doesn't matter. They sell all kinds of clothes in Las Vegas." It was at that moment that they noticed a Cadillac roar past them. Chuck Wilson was at the wheel.

"There goes that rascal. I ought to catch him and give him what he really deserves," said Kevin.

"No, no, Kevin. I think he's had enough. Your hand doesn't hurt, does it? It was a trip to see those surgeon's hands take on a new profession. I hope they're not hurt," said Africa, tickled but concerned. She had developed a new pride in Kevin, and she gently stroked his hand.

"Not this time, Honey, but I wouldn't want to do that too often. Just because it is hard on the hands. But, in a way it was fun, particularly under the circumstances," he said smiling. They both laughed happily as Kevin turned the car onto the freeway, and headed for Las Vegas.

Suddenly, Africa said, "Kevin, I don't understand. We're going to get married, but what about...."

Kevin interrupted her with, "My engagement?" He looked at her and smiled. "I won't let you have to ask me about that a second time." he continued squeezing her hand affectionately.

"Dad was the first person I met when I arrived home this evening. He asked me what had happened between you and me, because he really thought we were in love, and he liked you so much. I told him I didn't know, and because I hadn't heard from you, I had come home to see what was wrong. Dad shared that copy of The Tribune with me, the one with Nanette's picture, announcing the engagement which I knew nothing about."

"She didn't, Kevin!" How could she?" exclaimed Africa."

"It's been done before, Honey. At any rate, my mother was with her all the way. They both felt that rather than cause any embarrassment to either of our families, that I'd go along with their plans. Africa, I was shocked. Mom came in while Dad and I were discussing the matter, and when she found out I wouldn't go along with the game, she threw a fit. It seems that she and Nanette planned to get me home a day or so before the wedding, for which they would have made all the arrangements. They actually thought they could convince me to go along with them. Honey, when I pictured you reading that garbage, I was sick. I left the house immediately to find you."

Africa was surprised, but comforted at what Kevin told her. They filled each other in on all the details of the past few weeks, since Mrs. Hildenbrandt's death.

"That morning after I left you," continued Kevin, as he sped down the freeway, "I went to the phone, and took care of a lot of business. There was the mortician, out of town relatives, like my Uncle Benjamin, who has the hospital down in Atlanta, and a few of Grandma's real close friends. When I got back upstairs, you had packed everything and gone."

Africa told Kevin what had transpired between his mother and her. He was shocked and so terribly upset that he pulled the car off to the side of the road, to apologize for Gloria's actions.

"Don't bother to do this again, Kevin," she explained. "I've got lots more to tell you, and if you stop like this each time, we'll never make Las Vegas, for days." Their kisses held them up for a longer period.

Kevin told Africa how he had looked for her at the house after the funeral, and was concerned when she didn't show up. He was just about to call her, when a phone call came with news of his Uncle Benjamin's sudden heart attack, down in Georgia. He had to catch the next plane out, but took time out to write her a lengthy letter, telling her of his plans, giving her the Atlanta address, telephone number, and asking her to call him the next day, collect. He gave the letter, sealed, to his mother, with explicit directions for her to give to Africa.

"What letter, Kevin?" asked Africa. "She never gave it to me!" she exclaimed.

"I know, Honey. I know," said Kevin. "Just before I talked to Dad, I had looked in the hall credenza for mail, and possibly a letter from you, when I discovered my letter to you, stuffed in the corner of a drawer and opened."

"Oh, Kevin if only I had received it."

Kevin went on to tell Africa how disappointed he was when he didn't hear from her that next day, after he had arrived in Atlanta, and how that disappointment grew as each day passed. His uncle was gravely ill, and he was very busy trying to keep the hospital running, take care of his uncle's other real estate investments, as well as Uncle Benjamin himself. He called her long distance, but the phone was out of order. He knew how to get to her house, but had never remembered her house number, and her street was a long one, running clear across town. Finally he called his mother and asked if she had heard from Africa. She told him no. However, she said Africa had been over the day after he left for her check, and she had given Africa his letter.

"Kevin!" cried Africa when she heard what Gloria said about giving her the letter.

"It's all right, Honey. I know," soothed Kevin, with his eyes glued on the road. He tightened his arm about her, and continued, as she snuggled closer to him.

"I was so frustrated, Honey. Uncle Benjamin died after a few days, and Mom and Nanette came down to the funeral."

"So that's where they were going," said Africa, and then she told Kevin all about her last visit to the house, even the slapping of his mother. Kevin roared with laughter.

"That would have been worth money to see, Honey."

"I'm glad you're not angry with me," said Africa.

"Never, under the circumstances," he said. "It sounds like pay back to me. Well, I finally got Uncle Benjamin's business quiet after the funeral. He left me most everything, Africa, the hospital and the house. Just wait till you see it! You'll love it!

The house is red brick, colonial style, with white shutters, big white pillars supporting the roof and it has sixteen large rooms. It's on forty acres of land, with a small lake, that actually has fish. There's a pool, tennis courts, a hot house for plants, and a riding stable with fine horses. Willie and Nellie are the husband and wife caretakers. Of course there's other help too. Uncle Benjamin wanted me to take over the hospital and the house. You see, he left half his other assets to me, and the other half to Mark. He was anxiously waiting for me to finish my surgical training. The hospital is the finest, Africa. I could stay there and work day and night. So many people depend upon its services, and Uncle Benjamin hired the best staff possible. It's great, Baby, just you wait and see, cause that's where we're going to live and raise our family. Please want that too, Honey. That's where I want our baby born, Africa," he said smiling at her.

Africa kissed his cheek, tenderly. "I want whatever you want, Kevin, and to be wherever you are, then I'll be happy."

CHAPTER 14

 evin and Africa stopped at two Justices of the Peace, but there were several couples ahead of them at each, so they choose to drive further in their search of an ideal place to wed. They finally found just what they wanted, a quaint little adobe brick chapel, whose walls were laden with ivy and colorful wisteria vines.

Once inside, they felt transported into another world. The vestibule contained antique Italian furnishings, red carpeting, and dramatic paintings of the Virgin Mary, and Jesus with his disciples. After answering the necessary questions and signing forms, to the satisfaction of a sweet faced, white hair, little lady, they were ushered by a friendly, well dressed gentleman into a delightfully, beautiful waiting room to await their turn inside the sanctuary. There were only two couples ahead of them, seated in scheduled areas of the room which gave every appearance of a heavenly garden. Kevin and Africa sat close to one another on a white satiny love seat, enthralled with the beauty that surrounded them. There was a frothy fountain, which bubbled and spurted streams of multicolored water into a white, marble pool, alive with shimmering, tropical fish. The floor was a carpet of green grass, and gas lanterns provided a soft lighting for the flowers an plants, which blended into the exquisite wall murals, depicting paradise. Neither Kevin or Africa could differentiate the real from the make believe. Live love birds cooed sleepily from ornate, flower decked cages. A young woman harpist approached them from a latticed entrance, and asked requests for their wedding songs. Kevin rested his eyes on Africa, while she gave their favorite, "We've Only Just Begun", and then he requested, "You Are So Beautiful", as he drew Africa closer into the circle of his arm. The harpist withdrew a short distance, then began to ripple their tunes. Kevin and Africa listened, enraptured, to the melodious strains. Suddenly Kevin reached into his pocket with a start.

"I almost forgot, Doll, I've something for you." Kevin brought forth a little blue, velvet case, and handed it to Africa. "Go ahead, open it," he told her.

Africa squealed with delight when she opened the box, and found a sparkling diamond solitaire. Kevin removed the ring from it's case, and taking Africa's left hand, he gently placed it on her finger.

"Kevin, it is so beautiful!" Africa finally managed. "And it fits perfectly."

For the first time since she had known him, Africa caught Kevin shy.

"I bought it for you in Atlanta, Africa." He looked down at her finger, then into her eyes. "I was hoping at the time, you would like it, would have me, and wouldn't think I was taking too much for granted."

"Oh, Kevin," smiled Africa in happiness. "You felt that way""

"Yes, I didn't know if you were ready just yet, but I see I was right on time."

They both laughed, as Africa admired the ring in awe, and pride.

"I've got the wedding band, too. They match, came together," said Kevin.

"Oh, Kevin, let me see!"

"Not on your life, Girl. I hear that's bad luck. You'll have to wait a few minutes."

And to Africa, it seemed it would only be a few minutes, because no sooner than Kevin finished speaking, than the elderly gentleman beckoned him into an adjoining room. Africa started to follow, but was very politely, requested to remain where she was. A short time later, the man reappeared and escorted her into the vestibule, where he opened the chapel doors, and left her standing in the middle.

The sanctuary was beautiful, and although small, it bore all the solemn dignity of a lofty cathedral, with its rich mahogany pews, and exquisite, stained glass windows. Africa took two steps forward, and a burst of organ music, filled with the sound of trumpets, sounded throughout the chapel. It was "Trumpet Rejoice", played in all its glory. She saw the minister, dressed in his sacred robes, standing in the pulpit, and Kevin, tall, fine and handsome, awaiting her at the altar. Someone thrust an incredible bouquet of precious Phalaenopis Orchids with miniature ivy, into her arms as the organ again rejoiced with, "Here Comes The Bride."

Africa took her cue and moved slowly down the aisle in step with the music. Kevin watched her with pride. Her curvaceous, young body, transformed the white uniform into the loveliest of wedding gowns. She held her head high, and a tender, sweet smile parted her lips. The early morning sunlight was refracted into bits of gold and jewels, as it filtered through the stained glass windows, and sprinkled over her exotic beauty. Kevin thought Africa to be the most beautiful woman he had ever imagined, and when her large, sultry eyes locked with his, he knew, their love meant more to him than anything else in life. Africa reached the altar, and they were united as Kevin reached out to her, and tucked her small arm under his. He felt her tremble slightly, as her delicate, but graceful fingers rested on his wrist.

During the ceremony, Kevin produced the matching wedding band, with its brilliant row of five perfect diamonds, and slipped it on Africa's finger. The rings were so beautiful together, and Africa so overcome with happiness, that her eyes welded with tears. One tear splashed onto the rings, sealing the significance of their union. At the conclusion of the ceremony, their lips met in a divine kiss of sweetness, tenderness and passion.

"You are the most beautiful bride I have ever seen, Africa," Kevin said as they left the chapel on their way to the car.

"Even in this uniform, Kevin?" she asked.

"You better believe it," he grinned. "You couldn't find anything to fit you better", he continued triumphantly. She made him promise, that if she died before he did, he was to bury her in that same uniform, which she would save for that purpose.

"Seriously, Darling, my profession means that much to me. I want to work at it, and be right there with you," Africa said.

"And I'm looking forward to your being the hospital's Director of Nursing. As a matter of fact, I'm counting on it," Kevin told her.

"O.K., O.K., I will, just give me a little time. Oh Kevin, It's so exciting! I can hardly believe all the wonderful things that are happening to us."

"Doll, we've only just begun," Kevin assured her, then met her lips with his in a tender but exciting kiss. The honks of the car behind them reminded him that the light was now green, and in the process of turning red again. They just made it through on the yellow, leaving the exasperated driver behind to wait on the next green.

Kevin drove to one of the most fabulous hotels on the Las Vegas Strip. Escorting Africa directly to the area of fine shops, he invited her to pick out a new wardrobe, which would include tennis wear, swim suit, daytime and evening wear, shoes, lingerie, matching jewelry, and whatever else she felt she would need for a brief honeymoon. Africa had a fantastic time shopping, while Kevin bought for himself in the swank men's shop next door. The clothing was exquisite, and by the finest designers. Africa felt she must be in heaven. Afterwards, they relaxed in the beautiful bridal suite Kevin had rented, while a waiter served them brunch. Africa had never been in such lavish and beautiful surroundings. After the waiter made his final exit, and Kevin took her in his arms, she could not help but shed tears of happiness.

"What's this?" Kevin asked.

"It's all so wonderful, Kevin. As I said before, I really can't believe this is all happening to me. It's like a dream and I'm so afraid I'll wake up, and ..."

He kissed her tenderly, erasing all fear, as their smoldering passions steadily grew. Kevin undressed Africa as if she were a delicate and priceless work of art, that he had never viewed before, and when she stood before him nude, his dark, heavily lashed eyes swept over her with adoring appreciation.

"Each time I look at you, Darling, you are more beautiful than before. A lifetime together will never be enough for me," he whispered. His hands gently caressed her soft, velvety skin, tenderly gliding over her curvaceous, firm body.

"I'm so happy that you love me, Kevin," she murmured. "I want so much to make you happy."

Their eagerness and desire mounted as Kevin carried Africa to the luxuriously adorned bed, with its puffy comforter, and ivory, silk sheets. Then with an almost insatiable passion, they consummated their marriage in the beautiful ritual of love as old as man himself.

Africa awakened in Kevin's arms. He had apparently been lying awake, watching her. They gazed into each others eyes, their souls bared and open, expressing satisfaction, happiness, love and joy. Africa gave a soft laugh as her arms tightened about Kevin, and his chuckle was deep and warm. His hand caressed her abdomen.

"I can't believe it, Honey. There's three of us here. You, Baby, and me. God knows, I'm the luckiest man in the world, and he buried his face between her breast, as she stroked his hair.

"Kevin, if I'm dreaming, I better not ever wake up."

They laughed and kissed again, then finally decided to shower, dress and prepare for an evening and night of excitement and fun. Two hours later, after wet shower kisses, teasing, and giggles, they emerged from their suite. Africa was beautiful and radiant beyond words, while Kevin was more

213

handsome, proud and happy than any prince could ever dare to be. Hand and hand they left the elevator, and excitedly joined others for a fantastic evening of glamorous entertainment and merriment in the fun capitol of the world.

For three days Africa and Kevin enjoyed the best of Las Vegas from the most delectable of meals, basking in the early morning desert sun, cooling off with a swim in the hotel's luxurious pool, dancing in the afternoon and into the evening to the latest combos, then enjoying an extravaganza of live musical revues at dinner. They laughed hysterically at Richard Pryor, were spellbound with Frank Sinatra, Stevie Wonder, Nancy Wilson and Linda Ronstadt.

They celebrated with wine and sodas, the latter for Africa, since both were in agreement that she should not indulge in any alcoholic beverages during her pregnancy. Together they had the time of their lives. The gambling casinos were unbelievably exciting, and they spent hours in them without realization of time. On the third evening of their honeymoon, Kevin brought reality into focus, when he told Africa that they would have to leave the next morning, early. She was surprised when he said that Mrs. Hildenbrandt's will would be read as soon as possible after their arrival back in Los Angeles, and that she was a beneficiary in the will. Kevin explained that it had not been read to date, since the family had agreed that they would wait until he returned from Georgia, to be present. Africa was shocked to learn that she had been mentioned. Kevin then revealed that his mother had been instrumental in keeping her from being notified, since she had been trying to find a way to disinherit her. Dr. Hildenbrandt, Kevin's father, had learned of this, and both he and Mark were quite upset, and had told Kevin upon his arrival home.

Next morning, Kevin and Africa packed their new wardrobes in equally new luggage, and proceeded homeward. Africa counted their earnings from the Casinos. Kevin had won two thousand dollars at the poker tables, and Africa had cleared three hundred from the slot machines. Her eyes were bright with delight at her amazing success, particularly since this was her first experience at chance.

"Where did you learn to play poker, Kevin?"

"Remember, Baby," he said, holding her close as he drove. "I graduated from Central High, and Wiley Hildenbrandt was my granddad." They both laughed as Africa snuggled closer to Kevin. They kissed, and the Mercedes sped towards Los Angeles.

Kevin drove straight to Africa's home, when they reached Los Angeles. Lucy was home alone. She was so happy to see them that she laughed and cried all at the same time, while helping them carry their belongings in from the car. She kissed Kevin several times, in welcome, and told him how happy she was to have him as a son-in-law. Africa found it almost impossible to entertain the thought that she ever preferred that she marry Chuck Wilson. Lucy was delighted with the lovely silk robe that Kevin had insisted they purchase for her. She marveled at Africa's new luggage, and the beautiful clothing she had purchased. Africa could not remember having seen her mother so excited before, as she asked them to tell her all about Las Vegas. There was no way out when she insisted that they remain for lunch, as they followed her into the kitchen.

Kevin mentioned that they were in somewhat of a rush, because they were due at his home at six o'clock for the reading of Mrs. Hildenbrandt's will. While Kevin was washing up for lunch, Lucy rushed rapidly about the kitchen preparing a quick lunch of greens, cornbread, fried chicken, potato salad, lemonade and her famous, fresh lemon meringue pie. Africa knew that most everything was left over from yesterday's dinner. She was proud, because she knew Kevin would have an unusual treat, since Lucy was a rare, old fashioned, real good cook.

"Guess what, Mom? I'm in the will!"

"Say what!" Lucy's eyes grew two sizes larger.

"I'm in Mrs. Hildenbrandt's will that they are reading at six o'clock," said Africa with a bright smile. "She thought that much of me, Mom."

"I know that woman's about to die over there, Kevin's mother. She must be having a fit! Like they say, what goes around comes around!"

During lunch, Kevin and Africa told Lucy of their plans. They would leave, as soon as possible, after the reading of the will, for Georgia, where they would make their home. At Africa's urging, Kevin told Lucy all about his late uncle's beautiful home, and the hospital he had inherited. Lucy had mixed emotions about Africa moving to Georgia, but was thrilled to learn of the comfortable surroundings her daughter would enjoy, and the new lifestyle that would accompany it. She was further consoled when Africa told her she would come home every two to three months, and that if Lucy wanted her to do so, she would send for her to visit them as often in Georgia.

"I can come too, Baby. After our little episode the other night, when I went running out of here to catch Billy, I'm cured. I figured, if I could run up there the other night, and survive, I could do it to go to work. Chuck Wilson has even given me back my old job up at the sanitarium. I'm gonna walk back and forth. I've even been to the store twice, Africa!"

"Oh, Mom, I'm so happy to hear that. I knew you could do it. So much good is happening to us. I'm still in a state of shock!"

Africa hugged and kissed Lucy and then Kevin.

"Well, we've sure had our share of hell, but the good Lord's done looked out for us," said Lucy as she pressed down her apron and smiled at the happy newlyweds.

The Hildenbrandt study was cloaked in an air of intrigue, anticipation and hushed whispers as Kevin and Africa approached its open double doors. They were still dressed in the smart, white jump suits they had worn from Las Vegas. Africa's dark hair cascaded about her shoulders, and her bright eyes swept the room. Kevin knew she was breathtakingly beautiful. He was equally handsome. The white suits were striking against their brown skins. Africa felt self assured close to Kevin and knowing that she was Mrs. Hildenbrandt. Everyone was there. Kevin's mother, Gloria Hildenbrandt, and Jeannie sat on a settee whispering, while Dr. Hildenbrandt and Kevin's brother, Mark, spoke softly as they stood on one side of the room's large fireplace. Grandfather Wiley Hildenbrandt seemed to be listening intently from where his picture rested over the white, marble mantle. Jose and Lupe sat in silence, seemingly staring at the intricate design of the colorful, oriental carpet, from their straight back Victorian chairs. Seated at the massive, mahogany desk in the far corner of the room was a slender, mustached man whom Africa surmised, quite correctly, was the family lawyer.

Dr. Hildenbrandt's and Mark's faces brightened when Africa and Kevin entered the room. They immediately strode towards them, with hands out stretched for friendly hand shakes with Kevin and warm embraces for Africa. Jose and Lupe stood with wide smiles, extended phrases of congratulations and best wishes as they welcomed the newlyweds. Gloria and Jeannie Hildenbrandt stared, briefly, neither making any effort at greeting, then quickly resumed their whispered conversation. Attorney Moran's coughs finally signaled them all to silence. Dr. Hildenbrandt ushered Africa and Kevin to the twin settee opposite his wife and daughter-in-law.

The reading of the late Mrs. Hildenbrandt's will proved both a shock and a revelation of personalities to Africa. Her interest was titillated as she observed gasps, smiles of satisfaction, and change of attitudes. As Attorney Moran read, it became clear that company stock and income property was divided equally between Dr. Hildenbrandt and his sons, Kevin and Mark. Lupe and Jose were assured their jobs with adequate pay raises for as long as they were able to perform. Provisions were also made for their retirement. Both were delighted. The shocks began when it was read that Mrs. Hildenbrandt left her library, all her jewelry, and one hundred thousand dollars to Africa. The Hildenbrandt home was divided with Dr. and Mrs. Samuel Hildenbrandt owning one half, Mark and Jeannie owning one fourth, and Kevin owning one fourth with Africa sharing in this one fourth if she were married to him within a year of the late Mrs. Hildenbrandt's death.

Each time Attorney Moran mentioned Africa's name, Kevin squeezed her hand. She dared not look at the women opposite her. Just their gasps of surprise and dismay were enough for her. By the time the reading was completed, Africa was weak with delight and shock.

"Dear Lord!" she whispered to Kevin. "This is incredible! I loved Mrs. Hildenbrandt, and I know she thought well of me, but this is beyond my imagination."

"It's no more 'Mrs. Hildenbrandt'," smiled Kevin. "She'll be 'Grandma' to you from now on. It looks like I've married a woman that's well off."

When both, Gloria and Jeannie, came over and hugged Africa, she nearly fainted. For the first time, that she could remember, she was speechless.

"We're so happy to have you in the family, Africa," said Jeannie.

"I make it a point of being good friends with my daughter-in-laws," said Kevin's mother, Gloria, with somewhat a forced smile. It was too much for Africa, and she broke into tears as Kevin led her upstairs to rest before their departure in just a few hours.

"You'll have to understand, Sweetheart," said Kevin, as he held her in his arms, and they floated on his waterbed, "Some folks can change attitudes quickly when they know the battle's lost. Just think, now, this is part your house too, and no one can ever restrict you from it. Mom would rather get along than pay you rent." Kevin shook with laughter, soft and victorious. "Grandma was indeed

221

a card. She fixed their time," he managed between gasps.

Finally Africa joined him, and they rolled and rocked with joyous laughter. Their kisses finally hushed their mirth, and kindled passions, which they released by making love. Both marveled that the thrills and pleasure they experienced together seemed more intense than ever before.

"Sweetheart," murmured Kevin, "our life together will always be beautiful."

"My darling," whispered Africa, "our love is forever."

Two hours later, dressed in light weight traveling suits, which they had purchased in Las Vegas for their trip, Africa and Kevin emerged from the bedroom. Africa was chic in light blue linen. She wore topaz earrings from Grandma Hildenbrandt's collection. Kevin wore a comfortable tan sport suit, which accentuated his virility. Jose helped him carry their luggage to the waiting car. There was no one else from the family around. When Kevin inquired as to their whereabouts, Jose told him they had all gone out together. He assumed it was for dinner because they asked that Lupe not prepare for them. Both Kevin and Africa kissed Lupe good-bye. Her eyes glistened with tears as she bade them farewell.

Africa and Kevin thanked her for the delicious dinner she had brought to their room. They made her promise that she and Jose would come to visit them in Georgia, and teach their cook how to prepare tacos. Jose drove them to the airport.

As they rode along, Kevin was quiet, as if preoccupied. Africa knew he was hurt that none of his family even said good-bye to them. She began to wonder if she had done the right thing by marrying him, if it meant complete separation from his family. She could not hope to replace them. Moving closer, she kissed his cheek, whereupon life seemed to awaken in him again, and he told her he loved her more than words could say. Their lips met, and parted only when Jose teasingly began to whistle a wedding march.

At the airport, Africa's whole family awaited her and Kevin. Moses was there holding Little Joey as Brenda all but jumped up and down with excitement. Billy was all smiles particularly after Africa told him the Cadillac was his to use, if he took good care of it so that it would be in good condition for her to operate on her visits home. She promised to take care of all the upkeep. Billy gave her a great big hug and kiss. He vowed he would definitely claim that football scholarship for college now. Brenda hastily told Africa how well Moses

223

was doing at the bank, and that he had received another pay raise. Moses beamed with pride, and shook Kevin's hand in appreciation, offering congratulations to him and Africa.

"You all gonna do fine. You just look like you belong together," Moses said with a grin, as he bounced Little Joey.

"The Good Lord meant 'em for each other the day they was born," proclaimed Lucy, smiling and beaming with pride.

Moses again extended his hand, this time past Kevin. Wearing a big grin, he said, " Good to see you again, Dr. Hildenbrandt."

Startled, Kevin and Africa turned, and there behind them stood Kevin's mother and father, Mark and Jeannie.

"Dad! Mother!" exclaimed Kevin. Then seeing Mark, and Jeannie also, he became even more excited. Africa had never seen this side of Kevin. She watched as they each embraced Kevin, and was again surprised when Gloria reached out embraced and kissed her too. Africa was so taken aback with the reactions of the women that she at first, reacted in the fashion of a rag doll. Glancing at Kevin, and noticing the twinkle of happiness in his eyes, Africa surprised herself, as she regained her composure, and responded appropriately to their overtures.

The gate opened and both families joined forces to wave them on the plane.

"I want to be there when the baby arrives. Be sure to call me in time!" cried Lucy.

There was a moment of surprised realization as everyone reacted to Lucy's statement.

"Baby? Are you serious?" cried Brenda.

"Say what?" laughed Moses as he and Brenda paused a moment to stretch eyes at each other in an incredulous manner.

"For real? You guys really having a baby?" yelled Mark.

"Right on!" laughed Dr. Hildenbrandt. Gloria remained in awed silence. Billy just grinned with delight and waved.

"We want you all to come for the christening," shouted Kevin. He looked proudly at Africa, then said, "O.K., Babe, let's get this show on the road."

Her sweet smile and bright, beautiful eyes were dancing with happiness.

"You bet," she answered.

Amid farewells, and blessings, they turned, arms about each other and rushed down the ramp to board the waiting plane to Georgia. Everybody knew they were in love.